AS THE FOUR WINDS BLOW

Isobel Blundell isn't looking forward to her special birthday. Her archaeologist husband, Douglas, is in South America, and she and their three children miss him sorely. On her birthday, Isobel's mother Ailsa, and sisters Kirsty and Dorrie, give her Douglas's gift — an airline ticket! Overjoyed, Isobel sets off for a holiday with him at the dig. But heartache, danger, conflict and tragedy lie ahead for the whole family — those at home, as well as Isobel and Douglas in South America.

JUNE DAVIES

AS THE FOUR WINDS BLOW

Complete and Unabridged

LINFORD
Leicester

First published in Great Britain in 1996

First Linford Edition
published 2017

A catalogue record for this book is available
from the British Library.

ISBN 978–1–4448–3398–0

Published by
F. A. Thorpe (Publishing)
Anstey, Leicestershire

Set by Words & Graphics Ltd.
Anstey, Leicestershire
Printed and bound in Great Britain by
T. J. International Ltd., Padstow, Cornwall

This book is printed on acid-free paper

1

It still seemed so strange to be waking up without Douglas at her side. Sleepily pushing a hand through her hair, Isobel Blundell leaned across to switch off the alarm clock on the bedside table, her eyes resting on the photograph that stood there. Douglas had included it with his first letter from South America. It showed him standing with the other members of the eight-strong team at the site of the sixteenth-century Spanish and Inca settlement they were excavating. Isobel reached out to touch the picture with her fingertips, as if doing so might somehow bridge the miles and bring them closer. Douglas was looking directly at her through the camera, smiling broadly, his blue eyes crinkling at the corners. Wearing shorts and sandals and a wide-brimmed hat, he looked tanned and fit . . .

'Mum?' Alasdair came in quietly with Teddy bounding after him, her bottle-brush tail wagging furiously.

'What's the matter? Why are you up and dressed?' Isobel asked her son in a low voice. 'It isn't daylight yet!'

'There're badgers down by the beck. I saw their tracks in the mud yesterday!' he explained in an eager whisper. 'If I go while it's still dark, I might see them.'

'All right. But I'll make you a hot drink first.' She smiled, following him out onto the landing. 'Is Robbie up, too?'

'No. I don't want him to come, Mum,' Alasdair replied solemnly, soundlessly starting downstairs in his thick socks. 'He's too little and he makes too much noise.'

'I doubt you'll need your binoculars today,' commented Isobel a few minutes later, drawing back the curtains from the kitchen window.

Although snow still dusted the moors, the dark sky was low and brooding. A chill, heavy mizzle was rolling down from distant Hawksbeard Crag.

'Dad says it's best to always take them. Just in case,' Alasdair said, drinking his chocolate as fast as the steaming liquid allowed. 'I wish he hadn't gone away, Mum.'

'We all do. And being away from us isn't nice for him, either.' Isobel straightened up from setting the fire and came to sit beside him. 'You haven't had another bad dream, have you?'

''Course not!' he declared, not altogether truthfully.

'If you do,' persisted Isobel gently, putting her arm about his shoulders, 'you're to come and wake me — understand?'

'I'm all right. I'm not a baby!' He wriggled away from her, stuffing his feet into his wellingtons. 'Dad *would* come back, wouldn't he? If we asked him to, I mean?'

'Yes. Yes, he would,' Isobel replied at

once. 'But it means a lot that your dad was chosen to do this job in Castildoro. It's very important work, and it'd be pretty selfish of us to ask him to give it up and come home.'

'I still wish he was here, though.' Alasdair pulled on his new padded anorak.

'Me too!' Isobel smiled as she wrapped a warm scarf around his neck. 'Now, away to your badgers. Be back in plenty of time for breakfast. And, Alasdair . . . ' she called after him as the boy and dog dashed out into the cold blue dawn light, ' . . . don't get muddy! You have to wear that jacket to school!'

★ ★ ★

Alasdair got back as she was dishing up breakfast, his new jacket soaked through and liberally spattered with slush.

'Do I *have* to wear this, Mum?' he grumbled later, tugging at the too-short sleeves of his old duffel coat as he

4

wheeled his bike from the shed.

'It serves you right!' Isobel replied briskly, pulling the bulky coat tight across the boy's narrow chest to fasten it. 'At least it's warm and dry. I don't want you being ill again.'

She waved as Alasdair set off on the two miles' journey from Chimneys through the hilly lanes to Ferneys Beck village school. When he disappeared from sight between the hedgerows, she turned to her younger son. 'Come on indoors, Robbie. It's freezing out here!'

Robbie came running, jumping and squelching, and they started up the steeply winding garden path. Above them stood the brownstone house with its three tall chimneys, which gave their home its name.

'Mum!' Robbie tugged at her hand. 'Can we make a cake today?'

'Good idea!' she agreed as she unlatched the door and shepherded him into the cosy kitchen.

Janey was still at the table, dawdling over her toast and a fashion magazine.

Isobel compressed her lips, glancing at the wall clock. 'Shouldn't you be on your way to school by now?'

'I've only a study period first thing,' her daughter said with a shrug. 'It doesn't matter if I'm late.'

'Yes, it does,' insisted Isobel shortly, beginning to clear the breakfast dishes. 'You'll find *that* out when you sit your exams next term! If you hurry, you'll still catch the bus into Cottingby.'

'But I *told* you, it's only a study — '

'Janey, I won't argue with you again!' Isobel interrupted sharply. 'Just go upstairs and get ready. And wash that make-up off your face!'

'Oh, *Mum!* You're so old-fashioned!' Janey protested, her jaw jutting out obstinately. 'Aunt Kirsty showed me how to put it on properly, and Amanda and *all* the other girls wear make-up to school!'

'It's fine for weekends,' said her mother, frowning at the palette of colours which had been her sister's most recent gift to Janey. 'But I don't want you wearing it to school!'

Janey scowled and complained, but she gave in relatively easily over the make-up. *Too* easily?

Isobel considered her only daughter's behavior a while later while she and Robbie were baking. Would the cosmetics be hidden in Janey's school-bag and the eye-shadow and lipstick re-applied during the bus journey into Cottingby?

Well, you know your own tricks best! Isobel smiled sheepishly, remembering how she and her sister, Kirsty, had done exactly that whenever they'd gone dancing at the village hall in Auchlanrick; where their widowed mother, Ailsa, and younger sister, Dorrie, still lived. But their antics had just been high spirits, whereas Janey . . . Well, there had been times lately when Isobel hardly recognised her daughter. Over the past couple of months, she'd changed from being such a happy, sunny-natured youngster to —

'*Robbie!*' From the corner of her eye, Isobel saw him stretching up for the jar of golden syrup. Even as she darted towards him, the heavy glass jar tumbled from his small hands, smashing into smithereens across the stone-flagged floor.

'How many times have I told you not to do that?' she cried, snatching Robbie from harm's way, catching him into her arms and hugging him tightly. 'If you want something, *ask* for it! Now just look at this mess! Go into the sitting-room and stay there until I get the glass swept up.'

'But Mummy, I don't *want* to — '

'*Go!* And find Teddy and keep her in there with you. We don't want her paws getting cut on all this glass.'

★ ★ ★

The telephone rang while Isobel was still on her hands and knees mopping up syrup and splinters of broken glass with a damp cloth.

'Hi, Isobel!'

The link with Castildoro was poor.

Douglas sounded every inch of half a world away. 'I've been trying to call for two days, but you know what the phones are like here! Is everything OK?'

'Oh, I'm so glad to hear your voice! It's been — ' began Isobel emphatically, then bit her tongue. It was hardly fair to bombard Douglas with domestic ups and downs the very instant he telephoned. 'Yes, we're all fine!' she went on more cheerily. 'How's the dig going?'

'Better than we dared anticipate!' he responded loudly to be heard above the hiss and crackle. 'Yesterday, Angie — Angela Lennard, the young assistant I mentioned in my last letter? — unearthed a pot full of silver coins in near mint condition!'

'It must be very exciting!'

'Absolutely! I've been able to explore our surroundings a little now, too,' Douglas went on enthusiastically. 'It's beautiful country, darling — and you'd adore the tropical flowers. I'm sending some pictures next time I write.'

He paused, and for a moment neither of them spoke.

'I'm sorry I won't be there for your birthday,' Douglas said at last. 'At least Ailsa will be travelling down to spend a few days with you. And Kirsty's coming up from London, isn't she?'

'Yes. I'm looking forward to seeing them both — it's ages since we had a good natter,' she replied, although inwardly Isobel wasn't too sure that turning forty was cause for much celebration! 'I expect Kirsty will bring more presents for the children,' she went on. 'I'm sure she can't really afford it. And she spoils them dreadfully; racing about playing games, letting them do whatever they choose. Then when Kirsty goes back to London, *I'm* left trying to settle three over-excited children back into a sensible routine.'

'Kirsty's always been full of boundless energy, but I've never heard you grumbling about her before,' commented Douglas mildly. 'You sound as though you need to take a break.'

'How can I?' she demanded, her voice far sharper than she'd intended. 'I'm alone here with a family to care for and a home to run.'

'I wasn't . . . say anything . . . ' His sentences were disjointed, inaudible as the connection began to break up.

'Douglas, I can't hear you!' cried Isobel in desperation. 'Douglas?'

The line howled, and fell silent.

Regretfully, Isobel replaced the receiver, filled with remorse at having snapped at him. But Douglas had sounded so excited and carefree and happy, while she . . . Sighing, Isobel pushed a trembling hand through her tousled hair and returned to cleaning up the broken glass.

Wasn't Douglas missing her — missing their children and his home at all?

★   ★   ★

Kirsty Carmichael cycled through London's congested commuter traffic and

11

turned off the busy main road. As she freewheeled into the narrow street of tall Edwardian houses where she shared a third-floor flat, Josh Elliot jogged along the pavement beside her.

'You're cutting it fine!' He grinned. 'Aren't you going to Yorkshire this morning?'

'I'm bound for an out-of-the-way place called Ferneys Beck to celebrate my sister's fortieth birthday,' said Kirsty, her eyes sparkling. She liked Josh. Just a few weeks earlier, he'd moved into the flat she and struggling dancer Gwen Taylor had occupied since their student days. 'All I need do is get to Euston on time and catch my train.'

'Here, let me do that.' Josh effortlessly carried her bike up the steps from the street. 'How many gears has this got?'

'Fifteen — but I haven't tried them all out yet,' laughed Kirsty, unlocking the door. 'I rode it in a French sportswear commercial and afterwards had the chance to buy it quite cheaply. It was too good a bargain to miss.'

Pushing the bike into the alcove under the stairs, they sprinted up to the flat and Kirsty dived into the bathroom to shower and wash her hair.

'Gwen, have you seen my ski-pants?' she called five minutes later, towelling her hair. 'The beigey ones that match my top with the roses on? I'm sure I left them around here somewhere.'

'Borrow my new leggings,' Gwen called, pausing from her core strength exercises. 'They'll match your top. Middle shelf in my wardrobe.'

'Great — thanks!' Kirsty returned to her room with the leggings, casting an eye over the assortment of clothes strewn across her bed. 'I'm just wondering if I've got everything . . . '

'Enough for a world tour, I'd say!' Josh commented wryly, looking around the open door. 'May I come in?'

'Mmm, sure. Oh, could you pass me those two books from the shelf behind you?'

Josh handed her the paperbacks, glancing along the other titles crammed onto the shelf. 'Thackeray, Hugo, Brontë, Wilde . . . I didn't even know you *liked* reading.'

'Oh, I'm a real bookworm.' She beamed, squeezing the books into her holdall. 'I don't get nearly as much time to read as I'd like.'

'My boss has commissioned adaptations of about a dozen classic novels for the audio series we're releasing next year.'

'Oh?' Kirsty queried a shade distractedly. She knew Josh was a sound engineer with one of the small independent recording companies, but that was about all. 'Hmm, let's see . . . I've got Izzie's present, and Alasdair's bird things. Lavender water for Mum. But there's still Janey's to go in . . . ' She considered the floppy hippy-chick hat she'd bought for her niece. 'This'll get crushed if I pack it — I'll just have to wear it. Then there are *these!*' She brandished a tiny pair of multicoloured roller boots. 'Snazzy, eh? They're for Robbie.' Kirsty giggled, spinning the red plastic wheels. 'I'd whizz along to the Tube in a flash on a set of these!'

'Talking of which, how *are* you getting to Euston?' Josh asked, lending his weight to the bulging suitcase Kirsty was attempting to close.

'I'll call a taxi.'

'You'll never make it by car. I'll be glad to take you.'

'We-ll, thanks, but . . . ' Kirsty hesitated at the prospect of weaving, laden with luggage, across London in the rush hour on the back of Josh's motorcycle.

'Do you want to catch your train or not?' he persisted with a challenging grin. 'When I first came to London, I worked as a courier. There isn't a shortcut I don't know!'

★ ★ ★

Josh was as good as his word, and they reached Euston in plenty of time. He accompanied Kirsty to her carriage, helping her stow her bags and sitting beside her. Now the rush was over, there didn't seem much to say.

'I'm doing a session with a choral group today,' he commented at length.

'That'll make a change from heavy metal,' she returned with a teasing smile.

'*Quieter*, anyhow!' he agreed, adding lightly, 'you won't forget to come back to us, will you?'

'With *Violetta* coming up? No way!' she retorted, laughing when she saw Josh's blank expression. 'Oh, of course! You don't know about it, do you? There's to be a television version of Alexander Dumas's *Lady of the Camellias*, and Ruth — my agent — has managed to get me an audition.'

'Fantastic!' exclaimed Josh, genuinely delighted for her. 'You'd be great as Violetta.'

'That's kind of you,' she replied warmly, touching his arm. 'Since I started acting, this is the biggest opportunity I've ever had. I'll need to work hard to make the most of it.' She raised an eyebrow, indicating her bulging holdall. 'I have copies of the script, the play, the novel in French, the novel in English, and a video of the Hollywood silent movie. And my niece, Janey, has offered to coach me while I'm at Chimneys — so I'll be nothing if not prepared. I *want* this role, Josh! I really want it,' she confided earnestly. 'I can't seem to think about anything else.'

Guards were slamming doors, a whistle blew, and Josh rose hurriedly. 'I'd better get off, or I'll be coming with you!'

He paused, and quite suddenly Kirsty realised he was about to kiss her.

It wasn't just a polite kiss on the cheek, either. The warm tenderness of Josh's embrace took her unawares, lingering in Kirsty's mind hours later when she was settling into her room at Chimneys.

'Cold milk and gingerbread still your

favourites?' asked Isobel, appearing with a tempting tray. 'I thought we might have a snack and a natter. Mum has commandeered my kitchen.'

Kirsty looked up from unpacking her suitcase and smiled. 'Yes, please! Chimneys is the only place I ever taste home-baking.' She cleared a space on the bed so they could sit down. 'Isn't Mum looking well? It's a pity Dorrie couldn't have come down from Auchlanrick with her, though.'

'Graham won't let her out of his sight.'

'Quite right, too,' Kirsty chuckled, continuing more seriously, 'I hope all goes well for them this time, Izzie. They're longing for a family, and Mum will be overjoyed to have another grandchild.'

'Especially one living under the same roof,' put in Isobel, smiling across at her younger sister. 'It's lovely having you here again, Kirsty. I'm awfully pleased you were able to come.'

'Is everything all right?' ventured

Kirsty after a long moment. 'You seem a bit fed up.'

'I'm fine. Really. It's just, well . . . Oh, I know I'm being silly,' Isobel went on briskly. 'It's only that I haven't heard from Douglas today. I know telephoning from Castildoro is difficult, but I haven't even had a birthday card from him. When the postman brought an air-mail envelope at lunch-time, I thought . . . but it was from Douglas's parents in Canada.'

'In all these years you and he have known one another, has Douglas *ever* forgotten your birthday?' demanded Kirsty, going on to answer her own question. 'No, of course he hasn't. So he's not likely to start forgetting now, is he?'

'He's terribly busy and preoccupied . . . ' Isobel replied uncertainly.

But Kirsty just scoffed. 'Rubbish!' She turned away to rummage through her bags. 'Anyway, this is for you from me. Happy birthday!'

'Oh, thank you! I'll keep it till tea-time.'

Kirsty cleared her throat. 'Actually, you *might* prefer to open it now,' she suggested, her green eyes shining mischievously, 'while the children and Mum aren't around.'

Isobel's eyes widened. 'What on earth have you got me?'

'Open it and find out!'

Isobel carefully removed the pretty floral-patterned paper and opened up the box to reveal a frothy concoction of silk, lace and ribbons. 'A nightie set!' she gasped, smoothing her fingertips across the silky fabric and shaking out the folds to hold it up. 'You shouldn't have! It must've been ever so expensive. It's very extravagant . . . and frivolous!'

'Isn't it, though?' agreed Kirsty blithely. 'I got it in Paris. Do you like it?'

'Like it?' Isobel echoed. 'It's the most beautiful thing I've ever set eyes on!'

'Good! Now, why don't you take a long, leisurely bubble bath and get into the birthday mood?'

'I can't.' Isobel shook her head.

'Mum's busy in the kitchen, so I'll have to keep the children out of her hair, and — '

'Leave them to me,' Kirsty chipped in briskly. 'I'll take them out for a few hours. It's a glorious day. We'll have lots of fun.' She was already on the landing and skipping lightly downstairs. 'Enjoy your bubble bath and we'll see you at tea-time!'

★　★　★

'Close your eyes, Mummy. It's a surprise!' announced Robbie later that afternoon, taking Isobel's hand and leading her into the sitting-room overlooking the beck.

Opening her eyes, Isobel exclaimed at the huge iced cake, glowing and flickering with dozens of tiny pink candles.

'Gran baked the cake,' Janey told her. 'But we made the icing ourselves.'

'And the letters,' put in Alasdair.

'*I* mixed the stuff for the letters!'

Robbie declared proudly.

'That's why they're navy blue,' added Janey with a long-suffering sigh. 'He put in a whole bottle of colouring.'

'Navy blue is my very favourite colour, Robbie,' reassured Isobel swiftly, ruffling the little boy's hair and gazing at the heap of packages and homemade envelopes arranged next to her plate. 'My goodness, are all these for me, too?'

'They're from us and Gran, Aunt Dorrie and Kirsty, but these are from *Dad*,' explained Janey. 'He didn't want to risk posting them, so he gave your card and present to me before he went away.'

'This is from Douglas, too.' Ailsa Carmichael offered a bulky packet. 'He asked me to arrange it.'

Isobel's hand flew to her lips as she opened the packet and an airline wallet slid out onto the tablecloth.

'It's a ticket for me to go to Castildoro!'

2

Castildoro was drowsing beneath the hot morning sun, nothing moving at a pace any quicker than that of the weary donkeys laboriously carrying their burdens of oranges, sugar cane, cotton and cocoa beans along the dusty streets.

'It may be the capital city, but everything happens *mañana* in Castildoro!' Douglas Blundell joked, his arm about Isobel's waist as they explored on the first full day of her holiday. 'But it's never less than enthralling. Just look around you — so much history! Portuguese, Spanish, Inca . . . Did you ever see such a mixture of cultures?'

'It's fascinating,' breathed Isobel, hardly able to absorb the dazzling kaleidoscope of unfamiliar sights and sounds.

Douglas led her up half a dozen marble steps into the shady arcades of a long-deserted colonial Spanish mansion. Its crumbling verandas spilled tangles of vivid huge-petalled blooms that buzzed and hummed with insects.

'So how do you like Castildoro?' He smiled, drawing her closer.

Isobel leaned contentedly against Douglas's shoulder and exhaled slowly, drinking in the colours and contrasts. 'Even from your letters and photos, I never expected it to be quite so . . . foreign!' She laughed a little self-consciously. 'And somehow, it feels almost as though time has stood still here.'

'Castildoro is filled with echoes from bygone ages,' Douglas agreed, his suntanned face breaking into a broad grin. 'Including our hotel. But seriously, it's a very poor country that's only now emerging from over seventy years of dictatorship. During the regime of General Ortega particularly, all resources were channelled into strengthening the army and increasing Ortega's personal power and wealth.'

Isobel took Douglas's hand as they strolled onwards through the glittering sunshine.

'President Rosales is a good man,' Douglas continued, a frown touching his forehead. 'But there's an undercurrent of resistance to his plans for democracy.'

'Why?' murmured Isobel. She'd been deeply moved by the memorial Douglas had shown her earlier. Just a simple rough-hewn wall bearing hundreds of names, its niches offering candles, ribbons and posy tributes to the men and women who had given their lives during Castildoro's long and bitter struggle for freedom.

'General Ortega still commands a lot of support,' Douglas told her frankly. 'Especially in the military and amongst those landowners who rely on peasant labour to operate their plantations.'

Isobel nodded, holding tightly onto his hand as they walked across Castildoro's town square with its small white church and water fountain. A tousle-haired boy was standing on tiptoe to drink from the tin cup chained to the stone-carved pump.

'He reminds me of Robbie!' she whispered. 'I wonder what he and the others are doing right now?'

'Probably wondering what *we're* doing,' laughed Douglas. 'I wish we could have brought the children over — although I can hardly believe *you're* actually here! I was half-afraid you wouldn't use the ticket.'

'Mum had let the children in on the birthday secret and they were thrilled to bits about surprising me with it.' Isobel swallowed the lump which unexpectedly came to her throat. 'They helped me pack and organise everything. And they've all promised to behave while Mum's looking after them. Even so, I *was* apprehensive about coming,' she admitted softly, reaching up to touch Douglas's cheek. 'But now I'm here and we're together again . . . Oh, you'll never know how very much I've missed you!'

It was early afternoon before they returned to Castildoro's hotel. A Jeep driven by a pretty auburn-haired young woman drew to a halt beside them, and a man of around forty, wearing dust-stained shorts and a work shirt, climbed out. 'Douglas — wait!' he called.

'Karl! You haven't met Isobel yet,' greeted Douglas, his arm about her waist. 'Darling, this is Professor Karl Fischer from Clayman Groves University in New York. And Angela Lennard, his assistant,' he added as a smiling young woman came towards them. 'Angie, this is my wife, Isobel. We were about to find some iced tea. Won't you both join us?'

'Yes, yes, very well,' Karl Fischer agreed agitatedly, not even waiting until they were seated around a table in the hotel's lobby before turning to Douglas. 'The Soler brothers didn't show up at the site this morning. And one of our station-wagons and some of

our camping equipment have disappeared.'

'We depend heavily upon local
labour, Isobel,' explained Angela quietly. 'Enrique Soler is our foreman, and
his three brothers are amongst our most
trusted workers. Or had been,' she
amended soberly.

'This is totally out of character for
any of those men. As for them being
thieves . . . ' Douglas shook his head. 'I
can't believe it. We must talk to them.
Hear their side.'

'I drove out to their village. They
aren't there,' put in Angela. 'I'll have to
report the thefts to the police. I'll ask if
they know where the Solers are.'

Douglas considered for a moment.
'You might learn more by asking Sam
Fraser, Angie.'

Isobel noticed the wary glance that
passed between them at the mention of
the Scotsman whom she'd met at dinner
the previous evening. She understood
he was a pilot of some sort, and not in
any way connected with the excavation.

After Angela hurried away, the earnest discussion continued between Douglas and Karl Fischer, and it became evident to Isobel that Douglas was needed back at the dig.

'I don't want to leave you already,' he protested quietly.

She shook her head. 'Don't worry about that. While I may be on holiday, you have work to do. Besides, I'm not used to this heat yet. It'll suit me fine well to have a bite of light lunch and then relax for the rest of the afternoon.'

Suitably reassured, Douglas went off with Karl Fischer, leaving Isobel to her own devices.

The hotel proprietor had very little English and Isobel couldn't speak Spanish, so the two were muddling through good-naturedly as she tried to order lunch when a friendly voice spoke up behind her.

'May I help, Mrs Blundell?'

Sam Fraser sauntered into the dining-room, hanging his sun-bleached panama on the hat-rack, and she greeted him with undisguised relief.

'Please!'

In a matter of moments, Sam translated Isobel's order to the proprietor; and when he disappeared towards the hotel's kitchen, they both sat back and exchanged polite smiles.

'The food is better than you might expect,' remarked Sam while they waited for their order. 'Cooking is Hector the proprietor's favourite pastime.'

'Have you been staying here long?' she enquired conversationally.

'Castildoro and this hotel have been home for longer than I care to remember.'

Isobel returned his smile, and when Sam didn't say anything more, she mentioned the problems at the dig.

He nodded. 'Angela Lennard caught up with me at the airstrip. All I could tell her was that the site isn't the only place losing men, but I'll keep an ear to the ground.'

They continued to chat in a general kind of way about the dig and the country, and about Sam's work as a pilot.

'After leaving the RAF, I flew in Australia. On the mail-and-medicine run, as it was called back then,' he related wryly. 'Then I moved on to Oahu, ferrying tourists around the Hawaiian Islands. What a job *that* was!'

'What brought you to Castildoro?' asked Isobel, cautiously sipping a glass of the rough, sweet local wine that he had ordered for her.

'Oh, circumstances.' Sam grinned, dismissing her question. 'I'm still willing to fly anyone, or any cargo, that needs to fly. Although these days . . . ' He stared into the depths of his glass, the humour ebbing from his face. 'These days, I mostly while away my time swapping old stories and playing cards with Hector.'

★ ★ ★

Her conversation with Sam Fraser was still in Isobel's thoughts later that evening, when she and Douglas were walking in the fragrant coolness of the moonlit gardens.

'Mr Fraser hardly seems happy in Castildoro,' she said. 'And he doesn't have family or roots here. So why does he stay?'

'I've no idea,' replied Douglas rather shortly. 'He certainly seems to know everybody and everything that goes on.'

'You don't like him, do you?'

'There's something about him that just doesn't add up.' Douglas's face relaxed into a smile. 'On the other hand, he's well liked and respected by everyone I know, while Angie says he reminds her of Clark Gable.' He feigned a scowl. 'I'm not sure I care for you having lunch with a man like that!'

'Are you jealous?' replied Isobel coyly.

'Who, me?' he began, then laughed softly. 'Of course I'm jealous!'

Douglas bent to kiss her as they passed beneath the shadowy archway into the square; then as he raised his head his gaze fell upon the man in question. 'Speak of the devil!' he muttered drily, indicating the cantina where he could see Sam Fraser sitting outside playing cards. 'I ought to go and have a word with him, all the same.'

Sam answered Douglas's enquiry without raising his eyes from the cards. 'You've seen the last of the Soler brothers, your station-wagon and your camping gear. They were spotted heading south towards Vargas.'

'That doesn't make any sense,' Douglas countered stiffly. 'Why would the Solers leave their families and become thieves simply to travel two hundred and fifty miles to a place that's been a virtual ghost town since Ortega's defeat? There's nothing down there but swamp and ruins.'

'I wondered about that myself, so I flew over the place earlier this evening and took a look,' Sam returned. 'There must be nearly sixty men living under canvas on what's left of Ortega's old army training camp.'

There was silence while Douglas absorbed what he'd been told. 'Even if that's so,' he said at length, 'the camp's close to the border. Those men might be crossing as illegals and picking up lucrative work at the machine tool plant.'

'For all our sakes, I hope you're right.' Sam's tone was lightly mocking. 'Personally, I doubt it. And it's also my personal opinion — ' He glanced up for the first time, meeting Douglas's eyes steadily. ' — that you're a fool for bringing your wife to a place like Castildoro.'

* * *

Sitting in the north London rehearsal rooms, Kirsty kept her head bowed over the *Lady of the Camillias* script. At auditions, she found that watching other actors reading for the part only added to her nerves.

'Kirsty!' A tall man with a greying

beard edged along the row of wooden seats towards her. 'Long time no see!'

'Robert!' she exclaimed in a whisper. Robert Cox had been in the cast of Kirsty's very first play after leaving drama school. 'How are you?'

'Can't grumble,' he replied. 'Well, I *could* — but I won't!'

'Are you trying out for Alfredo?'

'I'm reading for the good doctor,' answered Robert with a wry grin. 'I'm far too old for dashing romantic heroes. Fathers, stolid businessmen and figures of authority are my line now.'

'You were terrific in that law series,' she responded sincerely.

'That show will run forever. I would've been in steady work until I retired, if they hadn't insisted on killing me off! No such thing as job security, is there?'

'No, there isn't,' Kirsty agreed with considerable feeling. She'd been fortunate not to be out of work for more than a few weeks during the past year, but Kirsty dreaded unemployment.

Aside from the financial anxieties, it was incredibly frustrating. She simply couldn't abide being idle and unable to work.

'Kirsty Carmichael?' somebody called. '*Kirsty Carmichael!*'

'This is it!' Kirsty muttered, taking several deep breaths as she rose from her seat.

'Just like hearing your name called at the dentist, isn't it?' returned Robert Cox with a sombre smile. 'Good luck!'

* * *

Kirsty trailed despondently up the three flights of stairs. The instant she shut the front door, the flat's dull emptiness closed in around her. Gwen was away for the summer season, and it was Josh's day for recording at the local talking newspaper.

She sighed heavily, kicking off her shoes and flopping down onto the orange and purple sofa. The room was horribly untidy; they'd been too busy this week to do much housework. Not that it looked attractive even when it was tidy, reflected Kirsty bleakly. The flat was rented. The ghastly furniture, too. It was practically impossible to rent a cheap halfway-decent flat in London without its being furnished.

She got up again, too restless to be still. Perhaps a trip to the gym to work out the nervous energy would do the trick. She was pulling a clean T-shirt and shorts from the drying line over the bath when the click of Josh's key sent her darting to the front door.

'Kirsty! What happened at . . . ' His words trailed away as he saw her crestfallen expression. 'Oh, sweetheart! Are you OK?'

'Not really,' she replied with a small smile. 'I could do with a hug!'

Josh opened his arms and Kirsty went to him, leaning her head against his chest. 'Do you want to talk about it?' he asked, stroking her hair.

'No,' she replied, going on fiercely, 'It's all my own fault, Josh! I made the fatal mistake of letting myself imagine what it'd be like to actually have the role.'

After another minute, she moved away a little, gazing up into his face. 'You're back early. Have you finished recording already?'

He shook his head. 'We'd hardly got started when one of the machines began playing up. I slipped out while it's being repaired. I ought to be getting back, but I don't like just taking off when you're so unhappy.'

'Nonsense!' she exclaimed with an immediate smile. 'Give me another hug, and I'll be fine.'

After Josh left, the flat seemed drearier than ever. Kirsty stood staring out to the grimy city street with its lines of traffic going nowhere and scurrying crowds trying to get somewhere, and in her mind's eye she could picture the space and freedom of the wild, windswept moors that rolled away beyond the windows of Chimneys . . .

Impulsively tapping out the number,

she waited some while before the telephone at the Blundells' home was finally snatched up.

'Aunt Kirsty!' gasped Janey, dropping her satchel onto the hall floor. 'Phew — I thought the phone was going to stop before I got to it.'

'Isn't Gran there?'

'She's at the bottom of the garden picking gooseberries with Alasdair and Robbie,' answered Janey briskly, going on, 'how was it? I told Amanda and all the girls about your audition today. I bet you got the part, didn't you?'

'I very much doubt it.'

'Did you forget your lines or something?'

'No, it actually went fairly well,' Kirsty replied truthfully. 'I did my best — but sometimes, your best just isn't good enough.'

'But we worked so hard practising your lines!' protested Janey indignantly.

Kirsty hesitated uncomfortably. She never flinched from facing her own failures, but letting down her family was always horrible. 'Even though *Violetta* has fallen through,' she began apologetically, 'I've got that part in the soap coming up.'

'Oh, yes.' Janey was indifferent. She never bothered watching the programme. None of her friends did. 'Hang on, Aunt Kirsty — Gran's coming. I expect she wants to tell you about Auntie Dorrie.'

'What about Dorrie? Janey? *Janey!*' But the girl was already gone.

Ailsa Carmichael picked up the telephone, her disapproving gaze following Janey as she flounced upstairs, her pretty face sullen. 'Kirsty? It's me, pet. Don't fret about Dorrie. She and Graham were pleased as punch when they called earlier. You'll never guess — Dorrie's expecting twins!'

'Twins?' Kirsty's happiness was tinged with concern. 'Is she all right, Mum?'

'Doctor Weir's satisfied she and the babies are doing well.' Ailsa sounded calm, though inwardly she wished she could be in two places at once. 'We've no cause to worry.'

'That's really wonderful!' said Kirsty warmly. 'Wait till Izzie hears!'

Ailsa sighed. 'I'll be glad when she's home again.'

'There's nothing wrong, is there?' Kirsty asked anxiously. 'You're managing all right at Chimneys?'

'Of course,' returned Ailsa impatiently. 'The children are being as good as gold.'

'They're super kids,' said Kirsty with a smile. 'Izzie's a lucky woman.'

'Yes, she has many blessings,' Ailsa murmured, fancying she'd heard a brief wistfulness in her daughter's voice. 'Having a career is well and good in its way,' she went on quietly, 'but isn't it time you started thinking about putting down roots of your own?'

'I'll admit there are occasions when I think of Isobel with Douglas and the children and a lovely home,' confided Kirsty, her gaze moving across the desolate, untidy flat. 'A place where she truly belongs.'

'I worry about you being on your own and living so far away,' Ailsa said gently.

'Oh, Mum, despite everything, I love my work!' Kirsty exclaimed fervently. 'I couldn't ever give up acting. I just couldn't!'

* * *

Douglas Blundell was never more content than when he was totally absorbed in his work. Isobel had long understood that, and took a genuine interest in what he was doing. So she was keen to see the site of the archaeological dig, which lay a long and bumpy drive beyond the outskirts of the city.

Isobel joined Douglas and the others in the back-breaking task of carefully scraping and brushing the stony, baked earth from what had once been the interior of a trading post. Occasionally she assisted Angela Lennard with the meticulous tagging, cataloguing and packing of the tools, pottery, Spanish coins and fragile Inca ornaments.

In addition to artefacts, a wealth of historical and archaeological data was being assembled. As Douglas observed, the dig was posing as many questions as it was resolving. 'Indigenous people had been living around that area for a thousand years before the Spanish arrived,' he was saying late one night when he and Isobel were driving back into Castildoro. 'So why was the place suddenly abandoned? Was there a battle? Or an epidemic?

'We're long on theories and short on evidence,' concluded Douglas, helping Isobel down from the Jeep and catching hold of her fingers as they started into the hotel.

'I can scarcely believe that in less than a week all this will be a memory,' sighed Isobel, gazing up at him. 'I'll be home in Yorkshire, and you and I will be apart again until Christmas.'

Douglas took her hand and tucked it under his arm, pulling her closer to his side. 'I hate being away from you and the children, Isobel. I wish I could come home with you.'

'If you've any sense, Blundell, that's exactly what you *will* do!'

Sam Fraser's curt voice came from directly behind them. Isobel and Douglas spun around.

'We have to talk. Over there will do.' Sam strode straight past them. 'We won't be overheard.'

Douglas and Isobel exchanged mystified glances, but silently followed Sam to the alcove with its musty couches.

'Why the drama?' enquired Douglas scathingly. 'What's going on?'

'Trouble.'

'Ortega?' Douglas's tone was abrupt. 'I don't suppose there's any point asking the source of your information?'

'You don't need to know. Just accept it's accurate,' answered Sam, turning his attention to Isobel. 'Our old dictator is staging a comeback, Mrs Blundell.

And he'll have the entire military backing him up.'

Isobel glanced wordlessly to Douglas. She'd seen and heard enough during her holiday to have gained a very frightening impression of General Ortega.

'The people who support President Rosales want to hold on to democracy, Isobel,' Douglas said. 'They've fought in the past, and they'll fight again.' His tone was urgent. 'You must go home. Immediately!'

Isobel stared at him, her heart pounding. 'I'm not leaving Castildoro without you,' she answered unsteadily. 'Either we both go, or we both stay.'

'Isobel, please! You're being unreasonable — ' He broke off, knowing she wouldn't be swayed.

The work at the site was at a crucial stage. If he were alone, Douglas would take a calculated risk and stay to continue the excavation. But with Isobel here . . .

'Take my advice — get your team

and pull out from Castildoro as fast as you can,' Sam advised, getting to his feet. 'And keep your plans quiet. The fewer people who know you're trying to leave, the safer you'll be.'

Douglas made his decision instantly. Transport here was basic and unreliable. Arranging travel, even in the usual way, took time . . . time they probably no longer had.

Douglas swallowed his pride and asked a favour from a man he not only disliked, but didn't wholly trust. 'Sam, will you fly us out? Isobel and I and any of the team who wish to leave?'

'I'll take you across the northern border. After that, you're on your own.' Sam moved away from the alcove. 'Meet me at the plane an hour before sunrise. Not at the airstrip, though. In the clearing beyond the cane fields.'

* * *

In the darkness before dawn, as she sat aboard Sam Fraser's plane waiting for

46

take-off, Isobel opened her handbag to look at the photographs of the children she'd brought with her from home.

'It's going to be OK, darling,' whispered Douglas reassuringly.

Isobel tried to smile. It had seemed unreal, terrifying — stealing out of the hotel and through Castildoro's deserted streets at the dead of night. The indigo sky above the distant mountains was illuminated with quick bursts of light and short explosions of sound. Fighting must already have started. The professor and Angela Lennard were flying out with Douglas and herself. The other five members of the excavation team had elected to remain at the dig and continue their work.

In the gathering half-light, Douglas checked his wristwatch. 'Think I'll go and find out what's holding us up.'

He spotted Sam Fraser standing some twenty yards away at the edge of the clearing, staring back along a narrow fire road between the cane fields. 'We ought to have left half an hour ago,' Douglas said tersely. 'What's the delay?'

'Spot of engine trouble,' returned Sam curtly. 'We'll soon be on our way.'

'Engine trouble?' Douglas repeated in disbelief, doubting Sam's integrity yet again. 'Then why aren't you working on it?'

His question was answered by an unlit vehicle approaching along the fire road. Sam waved it on, and without another word to Douglas sprinted back across the hard ground towards the plane.

An elderly gentleman was being helped aboard by his companion, a young man in his early twenties. 'My name is Bernaldez,' he introduced himself, murmuring graciously. 'My sincere apologies for keeping you all waiting. I am afraid I can no longer hurry — an unfortunate combination of old age and frail health. Perhaps this is the reason my grandson, Luis, has chosen medicine for his profession!'

Señor Bernaldez smiled at his own

small joke, however his grandson neither smiled nor spoke. He didn't even raise his dark eyes to look at his fellow passengers.

When the plane was finally airborne, Sam advised everyone to get some sleep. But Isobel found it impossible to rest. Her body was weary, but her mind was racing. She tried closing her eyes, and heard again those sharp reports that had accompanied them as they left Castildoro. Only now, the gunfire seemed closer.

In that same split-second, there was a dull thump. Nothing more remarkable than that — but the plane lurched and pitched.

Everybody was awake now. The cramped cabin was filled with shouts. Isobel heard Sam's voice from the cockpit.

'We've got a problem! I'll have to find someplace to put down.'

Douglas's arms tightened around Isobel and she tried to speak. But no words came.

In a rapid spiral of black smoke, the small plane plummeted from the dawn sky.

3

'Isobel! Isobel, darling . . . '

Douglas's anguished words gradually seeped into Isobel's consciousness. She stirred, struggling to open her eyes, but the lids were far too heavy. 'Douglas . . . ' she mumbled, striving vainly to dispel the muzziness. *'Douglas?'*

'I'm right here, darling. I'm fine. Everything's OK,' he reassured her softly, and she could feel his comforting hand smoothing her forehead. 'The plane's landed. We're down, safe and sound. Everybody's all right. Just lie still now.'

Isobel drew an unsteady breath, thankful it was over and they were alive and together. Her head was still spinning and she squeezed her eyes tighter shut, moving closer into the warmth and security of Douglas's arms.

When the dizziness finally subsided,

she looked up, blinking against the glare of sunlight shafting through the gaping doorway. 'Oh, no!' she gasped, reaching out to touch Douglas's shoulder and face, staring horrified at the blood on his skin and clothes. 'You *are* hurt!'

'Cuts and bruises, that's all. It looks worse than it is.' Taking her cold hands, Douglas chafed them within his own rough palms. 'Do you think you can get up now? We have to get out of here.'

Isobel heard voices and saw movement in the cramped cabin as Douglas helped her up the steeply angled floor to the doorway. With his grandson's assistance, Señor Bernaldez was already scrambling out, but Angela Lennard was still in the shadowed rear of the cabin. Propped up against one of the seats, the younger woman was obviously in considerable pain. Karl Fischer kneeled at her side.

'Perhaps I can help ... ?' Isobel paused in the doorway.

'No need.' Sam emerged from the cockpit carrying a battered grey metal case with red crosses on each side. 'Karl and I can manage. You get outside, and keep warm. Don't be fooled by the bright sun. The temperatures are pretty low at this time of day. Right then, young lady!' Sam continued, transferring his attention to Angela.

Once outside the plane, Isobel discovered that Sam was absolutely right. Despite the dazzling sun streaking the sky with vivid orange and pink, it was very cold indeed. A damp, penetrating mist was wisping from the slow-moving waters of a broad river snaking across the flat plain below. She could hear the distant trees alive with the shrieks and whistles of birds — but that was all. Silence enveloped Douglas and herself. Not a whisper of breeze, not a sound from the deep brown waters of the river. Not a single sign of human life, except the broken plane.

It lay behind them, a faint trace of acrid smoke hanging on the motionless air. Standing there together, gazing over the empty miles of plain, forest and hills, Douglas and Isobel were both struck with the same frightened thoughts. Douglas glanced down to her ashen face and tried to smile.

'All those birds!' He put an arm around her. 'Alasdair would be down there with his binoculars.'

'Yes! We must tell him . . . ' Her words tailed off, and in spite of the effort she made, Isobel's lips trembled. 'Oh, Douglas! The children . . . '

'They'll be fine. They weren't even expecting you back until the middle of next week,' he reassured her. 'By then, we'll both be on a flight home.'

'I can just imagine their faces, can't you?' Isobel leaned her head against him. Although she'd smiled, her eyes were bleak, and Douglas pulled her closer.

'I'm scared, too. I can't deny it,' he murmured against her hair. 'But the worst is over. If Sam had time to warn us he was making an emergency landing, he'd have time to send out a mayday call. Help is probably on its way,' he concluded optimistically. 'All we have to do is stay put until they find us.'

'I suppose so,' she agreed, struggling to get a grip on herself and stop shivering. 'I need to clean those cuts on your face and shoulder, Douglas. The first-aid kit is in my maroon holdall. Do you think it's safe to go into the plane and get — '

'I'll fetch it.' He hugged her again. 'And a couple of sweaters at the same time.'

Isobel held her breath as Douglas clambered back inside the wrecked plane. It lay at an angle on its side, the metal and glass crumpled and shattered like a child's smashed toy. She turned away abruptly, not wanting to think about what might have happened if Sam Fraser had been a less skilful pilot.

Cesar Bernaldez and Luis were sitting hunched on some coarse, bleached grass not more than three or four yards from where she stood. They looked as cold and lost as Isobel felt.

Luis hadn't uttered a single word during the entire flight from Castildoro, but now he was speaking in rapid Spanish. He was underlining the urgency of his argument with quick gesticulations, his lean face animated, his dark eyes earnest.

Señor Bernaldez was listening with great patience to his grandson's emotional outpourings. Occasionally he inclined his head or made a mild observation. Isobel realised he was simply allowing Luis to expend the fear and anger that were boiling up inside him.

Although frail, Cesar Bernaldez seemed to have survived the crash remarkably well. But an hour or so later, when Isobel had helped make Angela more comfortable, she was shocked to find him pallid and drowsy, his head slumped forward to his chest.

Luis was trying to rouse his grandfather. 'Don't!' shouted Isobel, stumbling over the scrubby ground in her haste to reach the boy as he raised a silver hip flask to Señor Bernaldez's colourless lips. 'Don't let him drink it!'

'I don't know what to do. Help him!' pleaded Luis. 'This is my fault. Because of me, this happens to Cesar! Please — *help* him!'

As a young wife, Isobel had taken a first-aid course being run by the WI, and in the years since had often had cause to be grateful for the training. But with Cesar Bernaldez she was out of her depth, and was relieved when Sam took over.

'Luis would have given his grandfather that brandy,' she reflected later to Douglas. Señor Bernaldez's condition had improved, and he was resting as comfortably as possible under the makeshift awning, which sheltered him from the heat of the afternoon sun. 'Giving anything by mouth — especially alcohol — could've been fatal.'

She poured water into Sam Fraser's tin tea-can and set it over the campfire to boil. Luis sat opposite, holding the old man's hand. Sam Fraser was with them, sitting on the ground and talking in low, grave tones.

'His grandfather said Luis was a medical student,' Isobel concluded thoughtfully. 'But he doesn't even understand basic first aid.'

'Hmm?' Douglas murmured absently. He was only half-listening to his wife's observations. He was concentrating hard on the map spread out on the dusty ground before him. How far north from Castildoro had they actually flown? And how long might it be before they were rescued? According to this map . . . He glanced up as Sam joined them at the campfire.

'Any chance of a cuppa, Isobel?' Sam grinned, but his tanned face was drawn, and there were deep lines around his eyes.

'I'm making some for all of us,' she explained, indicating the assortment of cups, beakers and tin mugs she'd found in the wreckage. 'There are the last of the sandwiches Hector packed for us, too.'

Sam nodded, rubbing his eyes with thumb and forefinger. It was the first sign of weariness he'd shown, and Isobel felt suddenly ashamed. While she and the others had been resting, Sam hadn't once allowed himself a break. The strain of the crash-landing, and the responsibility he obviously felt towards his passengers, had to be exacting a tremendous toll.

'Here you are,' she said quietly, placing the tin mug into his hands.

'Thanks. We've adequate dry provisions on board to tide us over,' he commented thoughtfully, glancing past her to the aircraft. 'Fresh water won't be a problem. Not in this area, at least.'

'How is Señor Bernaldez?' enquired Isobel after another moment.

'Not good,' answered Sam candidly. 'But old and sick as he is, he's probably got more strength and courage than the rest of us put together. He says he'll be ready to move on in the morning, and I don't doubt it.'

'Move on?' Douglas echoed sceptically, getting to his feet. 'Where to? And why? Surely it makes more sense to stay with the plane? A search party will sight the wreckage far more easily than it'll spot us wandering across country.'

'And who exactly do you imagine is going to be out looking for us?' demanded Sam sarcastically, fatigue quickening his temper. 'This isn't Europe, Doug! There're no RAF helicopters and emergency services waiting to come rushing to our rescue out here.'

'I do realise that.' Douglas stared levelly at him, his distrust of the man resurfacing. 'But you *did* have time to radio a distress message before the accident, didn't you?'

'For pity's sake, use your head! It wasn't an accident that brought us down. Or engine failure, or pilot error either!' exploded Sam angrily, tossing the dregs of his tea into the campfire. 'We were *shot* down! Whatever's happening in this wretched country, we're caught right in the middle of it,' he concluded bitterly. 'And if we're to survive, we have only ourselves — and each other — to depend on!'

* * *

Kirsty exchanged a cheery good-morning with the milkman as she jogged past his rattling float. Pausing for a breather on the seat beside the church, she inhaled appreciatively. She'd almost forgotten how cool and clean the air at Auchlanrick was.

The one-act play at Edinburgh had closed the previous evening, and on the spur of the moment she'd driven up to see Dorrie and Graham. Kirsty hadn't been back for a visit since the couple's wedding four — no, nearly *five* — years ago.

Before she cooled down, she continued on round the churchyard, past the manse, and down the hill again. The old grey house, where she and her sisters were born and raised, had scarcely changed. Kirsty felt glad yet again that after their marriage, Dorrie and Graham had decided to live there. Ailsa Carmichael was a sprightly woman with lots of friends, and she always kept busy, but she wasn't getting any younger. Kirsty didn't like the notion of her mother living alone.

Graham Nicholson's painter-and-decorator's van was still parked in the driveway alongside Kirsty's ageing hatchback. He was loading his ladders onto the roof rack as Kirsty turned in at the gate.

'I noticed your handbrake cable hanging loose under the car,' he commented, wiping his hands on his paint-spattered white overalls. 'I've fastened it back up.'

'That was kind of you. Thanks, Graham.' She got down on her hands and knees and peered under the car. 'Yes, I see where you've fixed it. I hadn't even noticed it.'

'Oh, it wasn't dangerous,' Graham replied. He was a solid, hard-working young man, slow to speak out and never one to make a great fuss. 'But it's as well to move it from harm's way, 'specially if you're to be driving over rough roads.'

'I'll certainly be doing that,' she laughed, straightening up and making for the house. 'I want to look in at Chimneys and say hello to Mum and the kids before I head back to London, so I'll be taking that short cut through the Scarswale Pass to Ferneys Beck tomorrow.'

She went indoors, and although the front rooms of the tall house were dull in the mornings, as Kirsty sprinted upstairs, sunlight was flooding onto the narrow landing from the wee back bedroom. It had been Dorrie's when she was a little girl, but Graham had redecorated it as a nursery almost two years ago.

Kirsty glanced through the open doorway to see her younger sister standing on tiptoe on a low footstool, stretching up to hang a brightly coloured mobile above the cradle. 'Dorrie — you shouldn't be doing that!'

'You sound just like Graham,' protested Dorrie mildly. 'He fusses, too.'

'I'm not surprised! You shouldn't be climbing about the furniture in your condition. Here, let me.' Kirsty took the mobile and carefully finished hanging it. Then they both stepped back to admire it. 'There. Oh, it looks super, Dorrie.'

'It came in this morning's post. I'd sent away for it. I know it's far too soon to put it up, but I just wanted to see what it looked like. There was a jack-in-the-box design, too. Do you think that would've been better than the rabbits?'

Kirsty shook her head emphatically. 'I'm no expert, but I don't believe there's ever been a baby born who doesn't smile when he — or she — sees a floppy-eared bunny rabbit!'

Dorrie laughed, sitting back heavily on the padded lid of the cream ottoman and gazing contentedly around the room. Then suddenly her smile vanished. 'You don't think I'm tempting fate, do you? Graham and I had this room all ready last time. And I'd knitted — ' Dorrie broke off, catching her lower lip between her teeth. She'd never confided in anyone, not even Graham, about the many times she'd crept in here and hugged that little matinee jacket to her, weeping alone for their lost baby. Graham had been a tower of strength, but it wasn't his way to show his grief. He'd never mentioned the miscarriage after it was over.

She said, 'You've heard the old saying about preparing a nursery — '

'You don't believe that nonsense, do you?' interrupted Kirsty.

'No. No, of course I don't. Not really,' answered Dorrie, her smile returning. She leaned forward to smooth her fingertips along the side of the wicker cradle, rocking it gently. 'It's just that sometimes, when I'm ironing or washing up or something, I'll catch myself imagining what it'll be like after the babies are born.' She folded her hands across her middle. 'Graham and I bathing the twins . . . putting them to bed . . . doing all the ordinary, everyday things . . . We've dreamed of having a family for such a long time, Kirsty. I just can't believe it's really going to come true at last.'

Kirsty gulped, swallowing the knot of emotion in her throat as she met her sister's eyes. Dorrie looked so very young — young and bonnie and glowing with the promise of new life. 'It *is* going to come true,' she insisted, reaching across to pat Dorrie's hands. 'And in just a couple of months, too.'

'Seven weeks and five days,' corrected Dorrie, her eyes shining. 'I tick each day off. They could've told us if the twins are boys or girls — or one of each — but I didn't want to find out that way. I think it's nicer to wait until you see your babies, don't you?'

'I'm not sure. I've never thought about it,' laughed Kirsty. 'Pregnancy suits you, Dorrie. I've never seen you looking happier.'

'I thought I'd never be happy again. But I am,' replied Dorrie simply. 'Oh, I *do* get nervous, though! Graham's taken on a lot of extra jobs so he can have time off after the twins are born, you see. So he's out from early till late every day, even weekends; and what with Mum being away . . . Well, sometimes when I'm on my own, I feel scared. It's silly, because if there *was* a problem while Graham's out,' she reasoned sensibly, 'I've good neighbours who'd help, but . . . '

'But it's not like having Mum here with you,' put in Kirsty understandingly. 'Is it?'

Dorrie ruefully shook her head. There was a big age gap between her and her two sisters. Isobel and Kirsty were already grown up and living away from home when their father had died, but Dorrie had still been a little girl. She and Ailsa had always been especially close.

'I'll be so much happier when Mum gets back next week,' admitted Dorrie. 'But don't tell her I said that, will you? I don't want her worrying.'

'Mum will still be worrying about us when we're collecting our pensions,' Kirsty returned, inclining her head to consider her sister. 'Have you had breakfast?'

'No. I cooked for Graham, but it was so early, I didn't feel like anything.'

'Have you any strange cravings for burnt toast and rubbery porridge?'

'No, I haven't!' exclaimed Dorrie indignantly.

'That's too bad.' Kirsty extended her hand to help her sister rise from the low ottoman. 'Because they're about the only things I can cook!'

★ ★ ★

'I've never had pancakes for breakfast before,' commented Dorrie later, narrowing her eyes across the table at Kirsty. 'You know, I think you could be

68

a really good cook, if you put your mind to it.'

'I don't have the chance. The flat's kitchenette hasn't a proper cooker. At least that's my story, and I'm sticking to it,' said Kirsty with a grin. 'Josh showed me how to make the pancakes.'

'Josh, eh? What's he like, Kirsty?' asked Dorrie conspiratorially, cupping her hand under her chin and leaning on the check-clothed table. 'You're really keen on him, aren't you?'

'Terrific — and maybe!'

'Maybe?' Dorrie echoed in disbelief. 'You get a funny look in your eyes whenever you mention his name. Have the two of you got plans?'

'Plans? You're as bad as Mum!' declared Kirsty amiably. 'Josh *is* special, and we'd love to spend more time together, but work keeps us apart. While he's in London, I'll be away doing a play or something, and if I'm in town for a spell, Josh is off recording, or producing in Europe. Mostly, we just snatch moments.'

'It must be awfully lonely. I couldn't live that way,' Dorrie said with a firm shake of her head. 'But at least you and Josh aren't married. I often wonder what Izzie was thinking about, encouraging Douglas to go off to South America. I mean, when she comes back from her holiday, Izzie won't see him again for more than six months! If *my* husband wanted to take a job halfway across the world, I certainly wouldn't back him up, the way she did with Douglas.'

'Yes you would,' returned Kirsty knowingly. 'If the job meant as much to Graham as working at Castildoro does to Douglas.'

Dorrie looked unconvinced, getting up to fetch a newspaper from the magazine rack. 'Have you read the article about Douglas in the *Cottingby Herald*? Mum posted me a copy,' she explained, leafing through the paper and folding it open at the right page. 'There're pictures of some of the things they've found at the dig.'

'Izzie's told me what Douglas was doing, but I haven't seen any pictures.' Kirsty began reading with interest. 'My goodness, no wonder Douglas is so keen! Castildoro sounds incredible, doesn't it? Imagine finding an almost intact room, with wine and letters and even a jar of pomade that belonged to whoever lived there centuries ago!'

Dorrie topped up their teacups as Kirsty continued poring over the newspaper. 'Mum sometimes mentions Paul Ashworth when she phones,' she commented when Kirsty returned the paper to her. Paul had been Douglas's best man, and was godfather to the three Blundell children. 'Apparently he visits two or three times a week, taking the boys to cricket matches, ferrying Janey to the ice rink and going to church with them, that sort of thing. Mum didn't really know Paul before, but she's got really fond of him.'

'He's a fine man,' Kirsty remarked evenly. 'And he's devoted to the children. Always has been.'

'Do — do you ever see him these days?' enquired Dorrie curiously.

Kirsty shook her head firmly.

'I'd heard about Paul coming home to take over the *Herald* after his father retired. But whenever I'm staying with Izzie, I rather think Paul stays away from Chimneys. Likewise, if I'm in the village or Cottingby, I try to avoid places where I might bump into him.'

'Surely after all this while,' exclaimed Dorrie, 'couldn't you at least be friends? You were inseparable at one time.'

'Friendship would be impossible,' Kirsty admitted at length. 'I hurt Paul far too badly for that.'

* * *

'I was a bit worried how these would wash,' Ailsa Carmichael was saying to Winifred Bell as she carried the bundle of loose covers in from the garden. 'But they've come up nicely.'

'Aye, they look grand!' Winifred glanced around from polishing the dresser. 'I'll give you a hand putting them back on, once I've dusted.'

She'd been coming up from the village twice each week to help in the house ever since Isobel and Douglas moved into Chimneys as newlyweds. Over the years, Winifred had grown to care for the Blundells and their children deeply — every bit as much as the family she and her husband, Harry, had always longed for but never had. Now she and Ailsa were getting the house ready for Isobel's return home from her holiday in Castildoro.

'Remind me to fetch those jam jars for you later, Mrs C,' remarked Winifred when she and Ailsa were zipping the chintz covers onto the sitting-room suite. 'They're in a tea-chest in the cellar.'

'Thanks. I used the last pot of strawberry in tarts for the children's lunch-boxes,' replied Ailsa, pulling the frilled skirts into shape. 'The garden strawberries aren't ready for picking yet, so Kirsty's taking the children

— well, she's taking the boys, as Janey flatly refuses to go — to the soft fruit farm along the beck.'

'Robbie'll enjoy that,' chuckled Winifred, stiffly getting up from her knees. 'He always eats as many as he picks. The farmer'll have to weigh *him* as well as the baskets!'

★   ★   ★

'I'll come to the village with you, Mrs Bell,' Ailsa said later, when Winifred was fetching her cardigan and bag from the cupboard under the stairs. 'I want to do a bit of shopping before I collect Robbie from playschool.'

'Some company'll make the long walk shorter.' Winifred jabbed a stray pin back into her wiry iron-grey hair. 'Because I swear these lanes keep getting longer!'

'Have you always lived in Ferneys Beck?' asked Ailsa as they strolled beneath the shady willows along the beck's winding bank.

'Except for a spell near Scarborough when the railway transferred Harry there, but that was only temporary.'

'How's your husband?' Ailsa enquired. Ill health had forced Harry Bell into early retirement.

'No better, Mrs C. Harry gets very down in spirit, too,' Winifred answered bleakly, starting up the slope of the narrow dry-stone bridge crossing the beck. 'He was always so strong and active. Now some days he can't even leave the house. It's hard for a man like him to accept.'

They were turning the corner by the village shop when Paul Ashworth's maroon car drew up a short distance ahead. He got out, walking back along the lane to meet them.

'Ailsa . . . Winifred . . . I was on my way up to Chimneys,' he began, then hesitated uneasily.

Ailsa looked at him curiously, waiting for him to go on. He frowned, glancing from her to Winifred and back again. She began to feel concerned, and watched the young man drawing in a deep, measured breath.

'Look — can we go somewhere? I need to talk to you both — and I can't do it here in the street.'

'What is it?' Ailsa's voice was sharp. 'What's happened? Is it one of the children?'

'No, no, nothing like that,' Paul responded hastily, trying to soothe. 'It's, well, a chap from Castildoro — a mutual friend of Douglas's and mine — called me at the *Herald* office,' he went on carefully, doing his best not to unduly alarm the two women. After all, there might be no real cause for concern. 'There's been some sort of rebellion, and this chap left Castildoro in a hurry. Douglas and Isobel tried to get out, too — but their plane never reached its destination.'

* * *

That night was hot and sticky; the steady rain had done nothing to refresh the heavy, oppressive air. Ailsa lay awake, listening to the hall clock striking each passing hour. Finally she got up, put on her dressing-gown and went downstairs.

Switching on the light, she pushed the kitchen windows wide open and went into the pantry. The rows of clean jam jars were still standing on the marble shelf, and next to them the strawberries Kirsty and the boys had picked.

All thoughts of jam-making had been pushed from Ailsa's mind by Paul Ashworth's news of Castildoro. 'Missing' was how Paul had described Isobel and Douglas's plane, she recalled, carrying the plump berries through to the kitchen and mechanically beginning to sort them. It seemed impossible to her that nowadays, with all the sophisticated equipment available, even a small plane could take off and just disappear. But then again, as Paul had said, it was a very large country.

He'd also said, trying to reassure and

comfort her and Winifred, that there was bound to be a perfectly simple reason, and the plane would turn up safe at any one of a score of remote airstrips. Although Ailsa hadn't said a word about Paul's news to the children, nonetheless she suspected young Alasdair had picked up that something wasn't right.

Suddenly, the terror Ailsa had been fighting to keep in check rose up, threatening to overwhelm her. She gripped the edge of the table until her knuckles whitened.

'Mum?' cried Kirsty in concern, padding barefoot into the kitchen. 'You're surely not making jam at this hour?'

Ailsa started, pulling herself together. 'The strawberries will be past it by morning. Besides, I'm better up and doing.'

'I'll help you.' Kirsty went over to wash her hands at the sink. 'Do you suppose Paul has got in touch with Douglas's parents in Canada?'

'Oh, good Lord!' Ailsa's hand flew to her mouth. 'I'd forgotten about them, Kirsty! I'd best phone straight away.'

'I'll see to it,' Kirsty responded gently. Her mother's jerky movements were conveying an agitation and anxiety Ailsa rarely displayed, and Kirsty went to her, drawing an arm about her shoulders. 'You look all in, Mum. Sit down and I'll warm some milk.'

Ailsa did as she was bidden, but shook her head vehemently. 'I know Paul said we shouldn't panic, but I can't help it. They're lost, Kirsty! Miles away from home in some foreign country I've hardly even heard of,' she cried, no longer able to contain her raw anguish. 'What if something terrible has happened to their plane? And Izzie and Douglas haven't managed to escape — '

Ailsa turned sharply, a slight movement catching her eye. Alasdair had come quietly into the kitchen and was standing rooted to the spot, staring mutely at his grandmother. She caught her breath, her mind racing. How long had he been standing there? How much had he overheard?

'Hello, love!' she forced a smile, trying to sound calm and ordinary. 'What are you doing up?'

Alasdair's eyes were wide. He'd heard what Gran had said and opened his mouth, tried to say something, but nothing came out. All he could do was stand there. His legs just wouldn't move.

As Ailsa rose and started towards him, Alasdair found his feet and his voice. He shrank away, tears brimming. 'Mum and Dad aren't coming back!' he shouted, recoiling from her. 'They're dead, aren't they? Aren't they?'

Turning on his heel, he fled into the dark hall. Wrenching open the back door, he crashed it back against the wall and tore out into the darkness.

'Alasdair!'

'It's all right, Mum.' Kirsty was already crossing the kitchen and running through to the hall. 'I'll go after him.'

She raced out into the wet garden, but Alasdair was nowhere to be seen. Kirsty stopped, peering into the deep shadows. Pitch-black grass, bushes, trees . . . Glimpsing a flash of Alasdair's light-coloured pyjamas moving swiftly beyond the hawthorns, she took off after him. She caught up with the boy near the beck and grabbed his shoulders, pulling him around towards her.

'Alasdair!'

'Why didn't you tell us?' he cried bitterly.

'Listen to me! Your mum and dad are alive and they're coming back!' she blurted recklessly, holding on fiercely to his shaking shoulders. 'Their plane didn't show up where it should've,' she went on breathlessly, falling to her knees in the rain-sodden grass so their faces were on a level. 'So we just aren't sure where they've gone yet, that's all.'

Alasdair's chest was heaving with exertion and rasping sobs. Tears mingled with the rain trickling from his fair hair and coursing down his cheeks. He said nothing, staring at her almost distrustfully. His body felt rigid, and Kirsty had to suppress an impulse to wrap her arms about the boy to comfort him. But she sensed such a gesture would send him shying even further from her. Slowly, she dropped her hands from his shoulders, half-expecting Alasdair to dart away. He did take a pace backwards, but stood his ground, making no move to run. His hurt blue eyes were locked unflinch-ingly onto hers.

'Are you telling the truth?' he demanded accusingly. 'Is that what's *really* happened?'

'Yes. The plane your mum and dad are aboard is missing,' answered Kirsty simply, wiping the sleeve of her pyjamas across her dripping face. 'Flights often get delayed or diverted to other places because of bad weather and all sorts of reasons. I think that's what's happened to their plane. They'll be all right,

Alasdair. You'll see.'

'Do you truly believe that? You're not just saying it because you think I'm not old enough to understand?' he persisted, his voice trembling. 'Mum and Dad always tell us things properly. Even really bad things, like when Mum had to have that operation.'

'If I knew anything else, I'd tell you,' she said earnestly. 'When Paul has more news, I *will* tell you. Everything.'

'Promise?'

'Promise.'

Alasdair studied her seriously, suddenly looking very like Douglas. He searched Kirsty's grave face a moment or two longer before making up his mind and nodding decisively. 'What do we do now?'

'Paul's trying to find out more information, but things in Castildoro are so tricky, he said it could be a while before we hear anything.'

'Tomorrow?'

'Maybe the day after,' she admitted honestly.

'Paul'll find out where Mum and Dad are,' declared Alasdair with absolute trust and confidence in his beloved godfather. 'Mum and Dad might even phone us from wherever they are, mightn't they? If they can get through, that is.'

He hovered uncertainly, shifting from one foot to the other, before taking a pace nearer. Kirsty reached out to touch his arm. 'Shall we go back inside now?' she asked quietly.

Alasdair nodded again, falling into step beside her as they started slowly back towards Chimneys. Ailsa was waiting and watching anxiously for them.

'I don't want to go back to bed, Auntie Kirsty,' murmured Alasdair, looking up at her. 'I won't sleep.'

'I don't think I will, either,' she agreed, slipping an arm about his shoulders. 'Suppose we fetch some pillows and quilts and stay in the sitting-room tonight?'

After they'd dried off, Kirsty made

up a bed for Alasdair on the sitting-room couch, while she and Ailsa settled into the fireside armchairs. It was after three o'clock, and Alasdair was curled up, his eyes almost closing, when the shrill ring of the telephone pierced the silence.

Ailsa was nearest and snatched up the phone. The voice she heard wasn't Paul Ashworth as she'd expected, but Graham's.

'Ailsa — I'm at the hospital.' Her son-in-law's words were clipped with shock and anxiety. 'It's Dorrie. She's — she's gone into — I think the babies are coming!'

4

'Dorrie was feeling tired, so she went to bed early,' Graham said distractedly from the hospital in Scotland. 'Then the pains started.'

'So the babies are definitely on the way?' Ailsa's question was brusque with anxiety.

'We're not sure yet. The doctors are trying to put things right,' he replied tautly. 'They won't let me see her. But they've said the next few hours are critical. In the ambulance, she was fretting about you being so far away, Ailsa. You couldn't . . . ?' He let the question hang in the air.

Ailsa thought quickly. Whatever was happening in South America, she couldn't help Isobel. But she *could* help Dorrie! She made up her mind. 'I'll come as soon as I can. Kirsty's here at Chimneys, so she can stay with the children.'

When she hung up, Ailsa's shoulders sagged. Three hundred-odd miles and several hours of travel were separating her from her youngest daughter. If only Auchlanrick wasn't so far away!

Alasdair heard her go slowly up the stairs and padded along the hall in his slippers to Douglas's study. 'Auntie Kirsty? Gran looked so sad I didn't like asking,' he began. 'But what's wrong with Auntie Dorrie?'

'You know she's going to have a baby?' Kirsty replied, hastily rummaging through the desk for a train timetable. 'Babies,' she corrected. 'They're not due for nearly two months, but Dorrie's been taken to hospital. Graham and Gran are worried in case the twins are born too soon.'

'What'll happen if they are?' Alasdair asked, his eyes heavy from sleeplessness.

'They'll be very tiny,' Kirsty answered, glancing up to see the worry on his face. She crossed the room to put her arm about his shoulders.

'They'll need lots of special care.'

'So Gran's going?' he murmured, his eyes large and forlorn. 'All the way to Scotland?'

'Mmm. But she'll only be gone a day or two,' Kirsty replied reassuringly, frowning as she opened the timetable. 'I can never make head nor tail of these things. Can you?'

'Oh, yes.' He nodded confidently. 'Dad showed me ages ago. I'll look Gran's trains up for you.'

'Thanks.' She perched on the corner of the desk while Alasdair sat dwarfed in Douglas's large winged chair.

'You write down what I tell you.' Alasdair slid a pad and pencil across to her as he ran a finger down the index. 'Gran'll have to change about four times.'

'Oh, here you both are,' Ailsa said, coming into the kitchen a short while later. 'I'm ready.'

'Alasdair looked up your trains.' Kirsty smiled, slipping the piece of paper into her mother's handbag. 'And he has a surprise for you.'

'Mum always gives us a packed lunch when we go on a long journey.' Alasdair handed Ailsa a bright blue plastic box. 'I made a flask of tea, too.'

'This is very thoughtful!' Ailsa stooped to kiss him. 'I'll be able to have a smashing picnic breakfast on the train.'

'You've been up all night, Mum.' Kirsty picked up Ailsa's raincoat. 'Will you be OK, going all that way alone?'

'Oh, I'll be fine. I just want to get there and see Dorrie,' replied Ailsa, watching Alasdair going ahead of them into the hall and out of earshot. 'Kirsty, we haven't heard a word about Isobel and Douglas! Surely somebody must know something?'

'I'm certain Paul Ashworth's right — it's just poor communications,' Kirsty responded positively, helping Alisa on with her coat. 'I've been trying to call Izzie's hotel since last evening, but I still haven't got through. The lines from Castildoro must be even worse than usual. The first train from Cottingby isn't till twenty past,' she went on, reaching for her jacket. 'But I think . . . '

Ailsa glanced up from checking her purse. 'What are you doing?'

'Going to get the car out,' she answered, taken aback. 'I'll run you to the station.'

'What about the children?' Ailsa reminded her, far more abruptly than she realised. 'You can't leave the children alone in the house!'

'No? No, of course not.' Kirsty shrugged ruefully. 'I hadn't thought about that.'

'We'll be all right, Gran,' said Alasdair, joining them at the door. 'I can look after Janey and Robbie while Aunty Kirsty takes you to the station.'

'I'm sure you can.' Ailsa touched his hair. 'But I've already called Mr Deakin's taxi from the village.'

★ ★ ★

Dorrie was in hospital some eighteen miles beyond Auchlanrick itself. Ailsa started up the steps with a mixture of relief and apprehension. What had been happening since she'd spoken to Graham all those long hours ago?

He was sitting in the waiting area, his hands covering his face, elbows resting on his knees. He glanced up at the sound of the lift doors opening and crossed the corridor towards her in a couple of strides. Tall and lanky, he looked very much younger than his twenty-four years.

'Dorrie's resting. I've seen her, though I don't think she knew I was there.' Graham rubbed his palm across his unshaven cheek. 'Mr Hamilton reckons she's out of danger — for the time being, at least.'

'Thank heavens!' Ailsa sank onto the plastic bench, suddenly weak at the knees. 'What — what about the babies?' she whispered, her eyes on Graham's drawn face.

'We don't know. Not yet.' He looked

away. 'There are all kinds of complications. She's very ill. The doctors were with her the whole night. I thought I was losing her — ' He broke off as the door of Dorrie's room opened. A nurse came out.

'Mr Hamilton will be along to check on Dorrie before he goes off duty,' Sarah Petrie said, smiling down at them. 'She's sleeping at the moment, but I can give you a few minutes if you'd like to pop in to see her. Only one of you, I'm afraid!' she added apologetically as they both got to their feet.

Ailsa immediately stood aside, but Graham shook his head, gesturing that she should go in. 'I'm rare glad you're here,' he murmured unsteadily. 'It'll mean the world to Dorrie to have you home again.'

Ailsa drew breath to explain she wasn't back home for good, but seeing the fatigue and worry in Graham's eyes, said nothing. Wrapped up in his distress for Dorrie and their babies, he couldn't be expected to think straight. He hadn't even asked after Isobel and Douglas's wellbeing yet, much less realised Ailsa needed to return to Ferneys Beck and continue caring for her grandchildren there. She merely touched Graham's arm and, thanking him, stepped inside the single-bedded ward.

Dorrie's thin face was ashen, her lips bloodless. She lay looking very tiny and frail, connected up to a battery of tubes, machines and monitors. As Nurse Petrie had explained, she wasn't awake, but while Ailsa was standing beside the narrow bed she stirred slightly, her eyes drowsily flickering open. 'Mum?' Her lips barely formed the word.

'I'm here,' Ailsa whispered, leaning over to stroke her hair. 'I'm *here*, pet.'

Comforted, Dorrie drifted into sleep once more. Ailsa continued stroking her hair, just as she'd done when her daughter was a wee child. Her heart ached at the thought of returning to Yorkshire and leaving Dorrie ill and afraid for her babies, but she'd promised Izzie she'd look after Janey, Alasdair and Robbie — and since Paul's news, those children needed her more than ever.

Sarah Petrie popped her head around the door. 'I'm sorry, time's up. Mr Hamilton will be along any second.'

Ailsa returned the nurse's smile, bending to kiss Dorrie's damp forehead before rejoining Graham outside in the corridor. 'She looks settled enough, and not too poorly,' she murmured far more optimistically than she felt. 'And she seems to be sleeping comfortably now.'

'That's a good sign. Dorrie needs must get some of her strength back. They've to do more tests later.' Graham sighed heavily, staring unseeing at the assortment of people milling along the corridor.

Presently, Mr Hamilton swept from the lift and passed the bench where he and Ailsa were seated, not appearing to notice them as he exchanged comments with the juniors at his side. The doctors turned into Dorrie's room; and as five, then ten minutes ticked by, Ailsa was aware of Graham glancing again and again up at the wall clock.

'Mr Hamilton's only supposed to be checking on her,' he muttered at last. 'What's taking all this time? Why doesn't he come out and tell us what's happening?'

Before Ailsa could reply, Nurse Petrie emerged from Dorrie's room. 'Would you come in, Graham?' she asked. Although her plump face was calm, almost without expression, there was no mistaking the urgency of her tone.

'But Dorrie's sleeping, isn't she?' he demanded abruptly, jumping to his feet. 'What's gone wrong? Is it — '

The nurse put a hand on his arm, firmly steering him into the ward. Before she followed, Sarah Petrie turned, her gaze catching and holding Ailsa's.

'The heartbeat of the weaker twin — the little girl — is scarcely registering, Mrs Carmichael,' she said quietly. 'I've a daughter myself, so I know what you must be going through. But I can assure you, Mr Hamilton is one of the best . . . Dorrie is in very good hands.'

Ailsa could only nod. Suddenly she was left quite alone with her fears, while beyond that closed door Mr Hamilton and his staff strove to preserve the life of her unborn granddaughter.

*   *   *

' . . . so I won't be home today, Josh,' finished Kirsty softly. She was sitting on the wide stairs at Chimneys, the telephone's wire laced through the carved balustrade. 'I'm sorry. I know you were planning something special for this evening.'

'Oh, no problem!' he responded cheerfully, but glanced in disappoint-ment at the welcome-home bouquet of flowers, the fine Italian wine, and the carrier bag of fresh fruit and vegetables he'd hastily dumped on the hall floor when he'd burst into the flat to answer the ringing phone. 'I'll cook you one of my fabulous dinners when you get back.'

'I'll hold you to that,' Kirsty laughed wistfully. Although they talked every day, and wrote long letters, these past weeks of separation had been an eternity. 'Mum didn't ask me if I could stay on here, she just sort of took it for granted. Besides, what else could I do? It'll only be for another day or two. But I do miss you so much, Josh. I was counting the hours until — '

'Kirsty, don't,' he groaned, 'or I'll be on my way up to Yorkshire in a flash!'

'I wish!' she returned with feeling, adding after a second or two, 'Has my agent been in touch? Ruth has my number here, but I thought perhaps she'd called the flat instead.'

'She might have. I left for the studios around seven last night and I've only just got home,' he explained, aware Kirsty was on tenterhooks about the prospect of a new job. Earlier in the year she'd had a few lines in a popular soap, and now a new, regular character was to be introduced into the series. Kirsty was desperate to get the role, and her agent had been pressing to secure her an audition.

'People don't like being pressured,' commented Kirsty uneasily. 'Maybe I should've asked Ruth not to push too hard.'

'She wouldn't have paid any attention. Besides, she's right to push hard to get you that audition. You're talented, dedicated, and you work harder than anyone else I know,' declared Josh loyally. 'Nobody deserves success more.'

'I know I'm lucky to be working regularly, and I do enjoy it — but I've had enough of walk-ons and bit parts and voice-overs and commercials,' she blurted, a familiar frustration gnawing at her. 'I really need this one! I want it so badly, it's all I can think about.'

'I know,' answered Josh simply. He'd shared the joys and exhilaration Kirsty sometimes experienced in her work, but he'd also held her close when she was feeling lost and defeated. He understood her; knew how vulnerable and insecure she really was. He loved her.

'You'll get the audition *and* the role,' he went on confidently. 'So when you do come back to me, we'll have a double celebration!'

'I'm — ' She broke off at the almighty thudding coming from the room above. Robbie had been in a monkeying mood since the moment he'd opened his eyes that morning. It hardly seemed possible that a single tiny person could create such chaos.

'I'll have to go, Josh — before Robbie and Teddy come crashing through the ceiling!'

★   ★   ★

She discovered boy and dog tearing around the bedroom, leaping from one bed to another. 'I thought you were playing with your train set, Rob!' she exclaimed, glancing to the toy box with its strewn contents. 'Come on, let's take it out to the garden.'

Robbie reluctantly trailed downstairs. 'I want to go to playschool!' he protested for the umpteenth time.

'Robbie, I'm sorry,' Kirsty replied, lowering her voice as they passed by the sitting-room, where Alasdair was fast asleep on the couch. 'But if I take you to playschool, I'd have to leave Alasdair in the house alone. And I can't do that.'

'I'll go and wake — '

'Oh no you don't!' Kirsty chased after him, scooping him up under her arm as he was about to burst into the sitting-room. 'Phew. You little monkey!'

But Robbie didn't return her laugh. He wriggled and squirmed. 'Let me go! Put me down!' he cried, his face cross and flushed as he struggled. 'I want Mummy! Want my granny! I don't like you looking after me! I want to go to playschool. Why can't I go?'

'I've already explained,' said Kirsty patiently, bundling him into the kitchen and closing the door firmly. 'Look, why don't you tell me what you do at playschool? We'll do it here at home instead.'

'Not the same.' He scowled, scuffing the floor with the toe of his sandals. 'We're making a castle today. I got all my cornflake boxes ready to take.'

'A castle, eh?' Kirsty hooked her thumbs into the belt of her shorts and knelt down beside the boy, who glared at her mutinously. 'I reckon you and I could make a pretty good castle.'

But Robbie was no longer listening. He'd heard a familiar sound and pushed past Kirsty, racing out into the garden and around the far side of the house.

When Kirsty sprinted round the corner after him, she stopped in her tracks. Paul Ashworth's car was parked at the gate and Robbie was already in his godfather's arms, tearfully pouring out his troubles.

With Ailsa being away, Kirsty had realised that seeing Paul again was inevitable. But her apprehension was instantly dispelled when she met his eyes and found not a trace of hostility there. Had he really forgiven her for walking out on him to go back to London?

'Auntie Kirsty!' Robbie hurtled towards her, his round face glowing. 'Paul's taking me to playschool! I'll get my castle stuff!'

'That's terrific!' She beamed at the child's delight, calling after him as he vanished into the house. 'Shout if you need any help!'

'Has there been any word from Castildoro?' asked Paul quietly, joining her on the steep path. 'Or from the Foreign Office?'

Kirsty shook her head. 'I called those numbers you gave Mum. They're going to phone back. The chap I spoke to was sympathetic, but seemed no wiser than us.'

'What they say, and what they actually know, are sometimes very different,' remarked Paul sombrely, studying her face keenly. He had no need to ask how she was feeling. The dark smudges beneath Kirsty's eyes told their own story. 'I may work on a country newspaper now, but I still have several contacts at the Foreign Office,' he went on. 'I could try cutting through the red tape to get some answers.'

'Oh, please!' she entreated. 'This not knowing anything is awful!'

'I'll see to it immediately I've taken Robbie to playschool.' He fell into step beside her and they started around to the garden door. 'How's Ailsa bearing up?'

'You know Mum. Somehow she always copes.' Kirsty smiled. 'Actually, she's had to rush back up to Auchlanrick. My sister's not well.'

'I'm sorry to hear that,' he returned sympathetically. 'Robbie was telling me that Alasdair's asleep and hasn't gone to school. Is he ill?'

'No, but what with one thing and another, he was awake all last night.'

'You've told the children about Isobel

and Douglas?' enquired Paul quickly.

'Only Alasdair. He found out accidentally. Overheard Mum and me talking,' she replied ruefully, leading the way indoors. 'As for telling Janey, it seemed wiser to wait until we know more.'

'If only we could spare the children this!' exclaimed Paul, following her into the untidy kitchen.

'Sit down, won't you? I'm sorry the place is such a clutter. This morning's been pretty hectic.'

Hastily, she collected the dirty breakfast dishes, unwilling to recount the tussle she'd had even getting Janey up out of bed that morning, let alone the row over her wearing high heels to school. Kirsty knew fine well how strictly Isobel felt about such things, but she hadn't had the heart to insist. Instead, she'd found herself watching as the girl stormed from the house, wobbling precariously on the black patent shoes.

'I haven't got around to clearing up

yet,' finished Kirsty uncomfortably, hurriedly collecting the jugs of milk and orange juice and pushing them into the fridge. 'Even *I'm* usually better organised than this!'

'There's nothing wrong with a house being homely,' commented Paul easily, nudging aside a panda and stack of colouring books so he could sit down. 'My place always looks so neat and tidy, you wouldn't think anybody lives there.'

Robbie thundered downstairs, dragging a brightly coloured rucksack bulging with empty cartons, kitchen-roll tubes and washing-up liquid bottles.

'That looks heavy.' Paul's serious expression relaxed as he smiled down at the little boy. 'I think I'd better carry it.' He glanced to Kirsty. 'Shouldn't he be taking fruit or milk or something for lunch?'

'Sorry!' She darted into the pantry. 'Won't keep you a minute!'

Paul was settling the boy into the rear seat when Kirsty joined them at the car.

'I'll make those telephone calls,' Paul said as he slid behind the wheel. 'Later on, I'll come over so we can tell Janey together when she gets in from school.'

'Thanks.' Kirsty had to raise her voice above the starting engine. 'For taking Robbie, and for all your help.'

He turned the key again, and the vehicle fell silent. 'Kirsty, I feel part of this family. You must know I'll do anything I can to help Isobel and Douglas.' He met her eyes steadily. 'And everything in my power to help you and the children.'

* * *

'I am to blame for us remaining here longer than is wise, Luis,' Señor Bernaldez reasoned quietly. He and his grandson sat with Sam at the edge of the makeshift camp the party had made beneath the shelter of the forest trees. 'We *must* go on!'

'You're not strong enough, Cesar!'

protested Luis earnestly. 'You have to rest.'

'No! There is not time, Luis! We have all heard military aircraft flying over- head.' The elderly man glanced towards their own wrecked plane, which Sam and the others had sought to camou- flage with branches and foliage. 'It is fortunate the pilots have not yet sighted our location.'

'Cesar's right,' put in Sam mildly, entering their conversation. 'We're on borrowed time. We have to make a move.'

'All right, all right,' conceded the younger man in resignation. 'But surely it's madness to try to get to the border? It must be almost a hundred miles through inhospitable country — ' Luis broke off, lowering his voice so it wouldn't carry on the hot, still air to the rest of the party. 'Castildoro is only three or four days' walk from here! Cesar needs medical attention,' he continued, inclining his head in Angela's direction. 'So does she.'

'Angela's arm is on the mend. She'll be fine,' remarked Sam shortly, beginning to lose patience with the argument. 'All this talk is pointless anyhow, Luis. You know perfectly well it's impossible for you to go back to Castildoro!'

'I am not afraid!' he spoke passionately. 'I didn't want to run away!'

'You're a young man, Luis. Your pride and sense of honour are wounded — this, I understand,' interrupted Cesar gently. 'However, you know you cannot return!'

'Neither can Cesar — or me,' Sam reminded Luis curtly. 'Not if we want to stay alive. Ortega will be looking for us, you can bet on that!'

'Because you both helped me escape my enemies . . . ' Luis sounded bitter and filled with remorse. He offered no further objections, and Señor Bernaldez drew in a relieved breath.

'I think we might now rejoin the others, Sam,' he said quietly, rising awkwardly and starting towards the bank of the stream, where the Blundells, Angela and Karl were gathered. The map, which Sam had given them, was spread across the hummocky ground.

'If this is our exact position,' Douglas began immediately Sam joined them, indicating one of the crosses the pilot had marked upon the map, 'then we were miles off our course. Why didn't you tell us that?'

'You didn't need to know.' Sam shrugged dismissively. 'Anyhow, we *weren't* off course.'

'Well, we certainly aren't where we ought to be!' observed Karl grimly. 'I think we deserve an explanation, Mr Fraser.'

There was silence. Señor Bernaldez cleared his throat politely. 'I asked Sam to change our destination. To cross the border at a different place.'

'And you agreed? Without consulting us?' Angela rounded on Sam. 'We hired you! Our arrangement was — '

'You *hired* me,' cut in Sam scathingly, 'to get you out of the country! I'll still keep my part of the bargain. The route I've marked on that map is the shortest way to the safest border. It'll be tough,' he added tersely. 'But I know this country. We'll make it.'

'You lied to us,' countered Karl. 'Do you expect us to place our lives in your hands again?'

'What choice do you have?' Sam returned coldly. 'You can't stay here, can you?'

'No, but we aren't as far from Castildoro as we thought,' Douglas said calmly. 'We can go back there.'

'That would be plain stupidity! Oh, for heavens' sake, I've had this argument once already today!' exploded Sam contemptuously, turning on his heel. 'Cesar, Luis and I are leaving for the border in one hour. Come — or not — exactly as you please!'

While Sam made his preparations, Douglas and the others began talking, trying to reach the wisest decision. Douglas distrusted Sam, and listened carefully to everything Angie and Karl had to say. And all the while, his eyes and attention were fixed upon his wife. She hadn't complained — Isobel rarely did — but unlike the rest of them, she wasn't acclimatised to the high temperatures or the energy-draining humidity.

Even in the shade of the trees, the heat was punishing. Isobel was visibly losing weight, and Douglas knew she was suffering frequent headaches and bouts of sickness. Why had he brought her to this wretched country? She should be safe at home with their children.

'What do *you* think, Isobel?' he asked softly, reaching for her hand. 'What do you want to do?'

'I don't distrust Sam the way you do — and goodness knows what might be happening in Castildoro by now,' murmured Isobel after a moment. 'But even so, I'd prefer going back there rather than trekking off into the unknown.'

'Me too,' Angela spoke up. 'My father

was a geologist with an engineering company, and we've lived all over South America,' she explained. 'I've a fair idea of what sort of country lies between us and the border. It'll be pretty hard going. Whatever the risks, at least Castildoro is civilisation.'

'And we're all American or British citizens,' Karl commented briskly. 'General Ortega would never endanger our lives. I vote we go back.'

'We're agreed, then.' Douglas rose and helped Isobel to her feet. 'We'll start for Castildoro as soon as we're all ready.'

A few minutes later, Angela was in the wrecked plane, sorting through her belongings. Fresh water for drinking and washing hadn't been a problem up till now — clear, quick-flowing streams ribboned the forest fringe. But from now on, they'd need to carry water with them. Probably enough to last until they reached Castildoro. They couldn't gamble on finding supplies of clean water along the way.

Ruefully discarding her meticulously kept journals, Angela was packing only the absolute essentials into her holdall when Luis climbed into the wreck. 'Allow me to assist you,' he said in his rather stilted English.

'Thanks, but I can manage,' she replied without turning around. 'There isn't much.'

'Even so.' He took the cotton-fleece sweater she'd been clumsily trying to fold one-handed, refolded it, and placed the garment into her holdall. 'Returning to Castildoro is a great mistake.'

'Is it?' she asked coolly. 'From what I overheard earlier, you wanted to go back too.'

'I have . . . personal reasons.' He hesitated. 'My father is still in the city.'

'I see.' Angela continued sorting. 'I'm sorry.'

'Professor Fischer is naïve to imagine that because you are American citizens, you will be safe. I am familiar with General Ortega. He is a ruthless man.

Your country's flag will offer no protection. Despite what you think, Sam Fraser is a good man. A good friend. You *must* come with us to the border!' he concluded, reaching out to touch her shoulder. 'Miss Lennard — Angela — there is grave danger in Castildoro. Please, believe me!'

'How can I?' challenged Angela, moving away from his touch. 'Neither you nor Sam nor your grandfather have been honest with the rest of us!'

'I — I'm not sure I — ' he faltered.

'Oh, don't deny it!' she exclaimed. 'When you and Señor Bernaldez boarded the plane, Sam pretended you were strangers to him — but you three know each other very well, don't you? And you and Señor Bernaldez were supposed to be simply passing through Castildoro. Nobody just passes *through* Castildoro! And you're certainly not a medical student, as your grandfather said you were. If that old man *is* your grandfather, which I'm starting to doubt! I like you, and I'd like to believe you, but how can I, Luis? *Luis,*' she echoed, with a despairing shake of her head. 'You've only ever told us your first name, haven't you? Is even that the truth?'

He sank down across the aisle from where Angela was standing, staring up into her flushed, accusing face for a long moment. 'I'm ashamed to admit you are correct about almost everything. I've known Sam Fraser most of my life — he's flown frequently for my father. Cesar and I aren't related, but he's an old and trusted family friend,' confided Luis frankly. 'I care for him deeply. And I'm not studying medicine,' he finished with a shrug. 'I'm doing post-grad history in Los Angeles. My younger sister studies there also. Fortunately, my mother was visiting her when the troubles in our country started, so they are both safe.'

'Is that where you're heading?' Angela asked, curiosity getting the better of her. 'Los Angeles?'

'Eventually.' He linked his long

fingers loosely, hesitating again before continuing. 'My name *is* Luis, Angela . . . Luis Rosales.'

'Rosales?' she repeated, sudden awareness leaping into her startled eyes. 'You're the son of *President* Rosales?'

'I am. But while my father remains in our country to fight for our freedom from tyranny . . . ' His voice fractured. ' . . . *I* flee to join my mother and sister in safety!'

'I can understand how you must feel,' Angela reasoned practically. 'But if you stayed, you might endanger your father still further. Also, if you were captured by Ortega's troops, you'd be an extremely valuable hostage.'

'My father voiced precisely those arguments to persuade me to leave,' he replied grimly. 'I accept their validity, however it is no consolation. I *will* return to Castildoro — but you must not, Angela!'

'What you've told me certainly explains a great deal — but it doesn't alter the situation for the rest of us,' she responded slowly, touched by the genuine concern in Luis's dark eyes. 'We *are* going back to Castildoro.'

★   ★   ★

Kirsty had pushed aside the sitting-room furniture and was working out to one of her aerobic tapes when the call from Ruth Goodman finally came. The theatrical agent had scarcely hung up before Kirsty was excitedly dialling Josh's number. Not since her mid-teens had anybody believed in her as Josh did. Kirsty was impatient to share her happiness and great good fortune with him.

'I've got the audition for the soap!' she cried the instant he picked up the phone.

'Fantastic! I knew you would! Congratulations!'

'I'm to read on Monday!' explained Kirsty rapidly, elation bubbling up inside her. After so many years of struggling and dreaming and being disappointed, suddenly — incredibly — everything she'd been working and striving for was at last within reach. 'According to Ruth, two of the directors saw me in that play at Bristol and really liked my work. She reckons I've a good chance of getting the role! Oh, if only I do, Josh! Me, actually on television twice a week — maybe for years! I can hardly believe it!'

'Well, I can. I'd give anything for us to be together right now!'

'Mmm . . . so would I,' she laughed. 'Mum's back from Auchlanrick tomorrow, though, so I'll be home for that fancy dinner you promised to cook. I can't wait to see you, Josh.'

Calling Ailsa and telling her the great news was next on the agenda. But there was no answer from the house at Auchlanrick. After several more unsuccessful attempts, Kirsty resumed her workout, scrambling to her feet when the phone rang.

'Josh? Oh, Mum, it's you!' Kirsty was delighted at hearing her voice. 'I'm so glad you've called. I've been trying to ring you for ages!'

'I'm not at home,' began Ailsa. 'I'm — '

'Hang on, Mum, I can't hear properly. I'll just turn off the music.'

'All right,' Ailsa sighed wearily. She was using the payphone in the corridor close to Dorrie's room. She'd scarcely left the hospital for what seemed like days, spending hours beside Dorrie's bedside or sitting in the hospital chapel. Thankfully, the crisis had passed. The scanner's indistinct images of the two babies, living and moving, had offered hope and comfort to Dorrie and Graham as nothing else could have done. But sometimes hope wasn't enough. Mr Hamilton had been realistic when he'd answered Ailsa's blunt questions . . .

'That's better!' Kirsty was back on the line. 'Mum, you'll never guess — I'm up for a part in a TV soap! My audition's on Monday. Ruth's already got the script, and my character's from

Rochdale, so I'll have to really work on the accent. I'm going to study recordings of some Gracie Fields's interviews to get the speech rhythms.' She paused, suddenly aware Ailsa hadn't responded to her amazing news at all. 'Mum? Are you still there?'

'I'm still here,' replied Ailsa shortly. 'I dare say it's all very thrilling for you, Kirsty, but I'm wondering if you're even going to ask after your sister.'

'Sorry, Mum! My head's in the clouds,' apologised Kirsty at once, regretting her thoughtlessness. 'How is Dorrie?'

'Her condition's stabilised, but she's still very ill. She might still lose the babies. The doctor was perfectly frank about that. The wee girl especially is at risk.'

Ailsa swallowed the knot in her throat and kept her voice even.

'I'm not leaving Dorrie. She needs me. You'll be all right coping with the children for a few days more, won't you?'

'No! I can't stay here any longer, Mum! I have to go back to London tomorrow!' responded Kirsty impulsively. 'Josh and I are having a special dinner together, and I need to get on with my preparations — I'm auditioning on Monday!'

'Yes, so you've told me. All you think about these days is yourself — and this part and that part. You don't seem to care about your family anymore!' Ailsa's voice was shrill and sharp. 'If this is what being an actress is doing to you — well, it's high time you grew up and saw sense! There are far more important things in life than gadding about with your boyfriend and prancing around on stage. I didn't want you to take it up in the first place. It's nothing but a waste of time!'

'That's not fair! Josh is a very special person, and acting's my job!' cried Kirsty, stung into retaliation. 'It means a lot to me — why must you constantly ridicule it? But then you've never understood. It was only Dad and

Granny Carmichael who encouraged me. You've never cared for me as much as you do for Izzie and Dorrie — I accepted that long ago. But I'm still your daughter!' she went on bitterly. 'I know I didn't do what you expected of me — get married and have children — but doesn't it matter if I'm happy or not?'

'This isn't — ' cut in Ailsa, but Kirsty's emotions were boiling over and she couldn't be silenced.

'Nothing — nobody — is going to stop me going to that audition!' she concluded, breathless and trembling as she moved to slam down the phone. 'This is the opportunity of a lifetime. Come what may, I'm taking it!'

5

The crash of the telephone slamming down ended Kirsty's conversation with her mother. But even as her trembling fingers were uncurling from the receiver, the appalling realisation of what she'd done — what she'd said — hit her. When would she ever learn to think before she spoke?

Clumsy in her haste, Kirsty dialled the house at Auchlanrick, waiting impatiently while the phone rang and rang. Why on earth didn't her mother answer? But, of course, she'd been phoning from the hospital. There was no way of reaching her. No way of explaining, of making amends . . .

Kirsty shivered, chilled after her workout, and started upstairs for a hot shower. She'd need to call Josh, too; let him know she wouldn't be home tomorrow after all. She halted on the landing as she heard Janey's angry shouting and Alasdair's usually quiet voice raised above the blaring television.

Racing downstairs again, Kirsty burst into the kitchen. Alasdair was at the large table, surrounded by his books. Janey was standing in the middle of the floor, hands on hips, her face white with anger. The portable television was at full volume and the tap was gushing steaming water into the sink. Brother and sister were arguing so furiously they weren't even aware Kirsty had entered.

'Quiet!' she shouted. 'What's going on?'

'He won't-'

'Look what she's — '

'Who was in here first?' interrupted Kirsty, snapping off the television and turning off the water. 'Alasdair, what's happened?'

'That's not fair!' cried her niece petulantly. 'Everybody always takes *his* side!'

'Janey, you'll have your turn to explain in a minute,' returned Kirsty shortly. 'Alasdair?'

The boy flushed, lowering his eyes and remaining silent.

'I asked you a question!'

'I wanted Janey to turn down the TV because I was doing my homework,' he mumbled uncomfortably, fiddling with the corner of an atlas. 'But she turned it up louder instead.'

'It's my favourite programme!' Janey was unable to hold her tongue a second longer. 'I wanted to watch it!'

'You *weren't* watching it!' he retorted accusingly. 'You were messing about at the sink!'

'I'm washing my skating dress! And you shouldn't be in here, anyhow. Why don't you go to your room?'

'Robbie's painting. I don't want him to splash my books!'

'Why not go into the sitting-room then?'

'That's enough!' Kirsty's voice was sharp. 'I was working out in there and I

125

haven't put the furniture back yet.'

'I'll help you,' said Janey, adding rudely, 'then *he* can go in and stay in!'

'I untidied it, so I'll tidy it up again. But I must change first. Meanwhile, would you like to work in the study, Alasdair?'

He nodded enthusiastically and started to pack up his books. His father's study was his favourite room in the whole house, and usually nobody was allowed in there. 'After I finish my maths, I'm going to draw a big map of Castildoro and the surrounding country. I want to mark where Paul told us the plane landed.' He hesitated, glancing up at Kirsty. 'I — I thought once they found the plane, Mum and Dad would be coming home, but they haven't — '

'Can't you shut up about it?' Janey's grey eyes were glinting. 'You bore everybody stiff with what you've read about Castildoro! Can't you understand there's no point? Mum and Dad'll be home soon. What good will your stupid map be then?'

Alasdair flinched as though she'd slapped him, but didn't reply. Janey turned pointedly to Kirsty. 'Aunt Kirsty, will this coffee stain wash out? I need my dress for tonight.'

'Are you going skating this evening?' she asked in concern, examining the dark splash on the short, full skirt. 'Is Paul driving you? No? Then I don't think you ought to go.'

'But I've already told Amanda!' her niece retorted, her eyes narrowing.

'It'll be after dark when you're coming home on the bus,' Kirsty said, shaking her head. 'Besides, you've school tomorrow.'

'I won't be late. Promise,' insisted Janey. 'Amanda's brother will bring us home in his car. Marcus is eighteen, and he's just starting working part-time at the rink's coffee bar.'

'So *that's* why you've been hanging around there, and at the Braithwaite farm,' Alasdair commented matter-of-factly, scraping back his chair. 'You want Marcus Braithwaite to take you to the school dance.'

Janey's mouth dropped open and her cheeks flamed. 'You horrible little . . . '

Alasdair was already turning into the hall, and Kirsty raised a hand as Janey made to lunge after him. 'Let it be,' she advised sympathetically. 'Give me a moment to change, then we'll tackle that skating dress.'

'It's all right for me to go?' Janey asked cautiously, her expression brightening into a sunny smile when Kirsty nodded slowly. 'Thanks! I told Amanda you wouldn't stop me!'

It wasn't until Janey had dashed over to the Braithwaite farm to meet Amanda, and Robbie had finally tired himself out and fallen asleep, that Kirsty found a quiet moment to ring Auchlanrick again. 'Mum — I'm so sorry about earlier,' she began soberly. 'Of course you must be with Dorrie. And don't worry about things here, we'll be fine.'

'I'm sure you will!' Ailsa's response

was warm. 'I knew once you'd calmed down, you'd see sense and do the right thing. After all, you haven't any ties of your own in London, have you?'

They talked for a few minutes longer before Kirsty rang off, wandering out to the warm, dusky garden. Leaning a shoulder against the honeysuckle trellis, she gazed out at the silent moors and purple-shadowed hills. Staying at Chimneys meant being away from Josh, and thinking of him filled her with keen, aching loneliness.

★　★　★

'You look bright-eyed and bushy-tailed,' remarked Kirsty the next morning when Janey was first down for breakfast, 'considering the hour you sneaked in last night!'

'I did say I was sorry for keeping you up,' Janey said, grinning sheepishly. 'And it wasn't all *that* late!'

Kirsty raised an eyebrow, going through to the hall and stooping to gather the post. Her agent had express-mailed the audition script, and there was a postcard addressed to Ailsa about Robbie's new glasses from the optician in Cottingby, and several letters for Isobel.

'You should try to get home earlier,' advised Kirsty thoughtfully, wondering if she should start opening Isobel's mail. Douglas's, too. There'd be bills; all manner of household matters needing attention. 'Especially during the week, Janey.'

'All right.' The girl suddenly beamed, her eyes sparkling. 'Oh, I'll *burst* if I don't tell someone!' She lowered her voice, even though Mrs Bell was in the pantry and out of hearing. 'Marcus is going to ask me to the dance! I just *know* he is!'

'Can he do that? It *is* a school dance, isn't it?'

'What? Oh, I see what you mean. Partners don't have to be from school,' explained Janey excitedly. 'It's a really huge occasion. There'll be fifth and sixth formers from other schools besides ours, too, so hundreds of people are going. It's held in the ballroom at Cottingby town hall with a proper band and a buffet and everything!'

'Is this your first dance?'

'First adult one.' She nodded airily, confiding cheerfully. 'At first, I was dreading it! The other girls already had their partners, you see. And five boys — *five* — asked Amanda. I was scared I'd be the only one without a boyfriend to go with. But now I've got Marcus, and I can't wait!'

'Marcus Braithwaite?' Emerging from the pantry with a bucket and mop, Winifred Bell caught the tail end of the conversation. 'Aye, I've seen — and heard — him roaring through the village in that rusty old car of his.'

'Marcus is very proud of his car, Mrs Bell,' reprimanded Janey, putting on her blazer. 'He's told me all about it. It's a classic model.'

'And I'm a Dutchman,' sniffed Winifred, perusing the mail Kirsty had left neatly stacked on the dresser. 'Robbie's glasses are ready, I see. That was quick!'

'We'll pop into Cottingby after lunch and collect — Janey!' Kirsty broke off, glancing around as the teenager grabbed her bag and made off along the hall. 'What about breakfast?'

'No time! I'm meeting Amanda. We want to get the early bus and window-shop for dresses!'

'Hard to credit I was like that once,' Mrs Bell commented to Kirsty as the back door clattered shut. 'Have you got anything sorted for your audition?'

'No,' Kirsty sighed, regretfully eyeing the bulky script on the dresser. 'I'm desperate to do it, but going would mean I'd be away from Chimneys until evening. What with the children to consider . . .'

'After I bring Harry back from physio, I can hold the fort here for a few hours. And why don't you have a word with Kate Wakefield?' suggested Mrs Bell, adding when Kirsty clearly didn't recognise the name, 'tall and thin with red hair. Runs the playschool.'

'Oh, of course — the minister's daughter. Paul introduced us,' said Kirsty with a nod. 'D'you really think she'd help?'

'She'll be glad to. Kate's a grand young lass,' said Winifred, fetching polish and dusters from the cupboard. 'Why, between the three of us, we'll have you in that soap on the telly yet!'

* * *

Although the visit to the optician was quickly over, Robbie was distinctly subdued when they got outside, fidgeting with the unfamiliar little spectacles.

'Fancy going for a milkshake?' suggested Kirsty as they started along Cottingby's high street.

Robbie just sighed and shook his head dolefully.

'How about ice-cream, then?' she persisted, hoping to cheer him up. 'Great big ones, with lots of chocolatey bits?'

He shook his head again, staring at his sandals. 'Want to go home, Auntie Kirsty.'

'You're the boss.' She smiled, taking his hand and crossing towards her car. 'Let's go home.'

Even as she unlocked the kitchen door and Teddy came, tail whirling, to greet them, Kirsty heard Janey's and Amanda's voices. She glanced at the clock — the girls should still be at school! Then she caught the unmistakeable smell of cigarette smoke.

'Kirsty!' Janey jerked around, startled as her aunt flung open the door and strode into the sitting-room. 'I — I didn't think you'd be back — '

'Evidently!' snapped Kirsty, taking in the cola cans, crisp bags, fashion magazines and sweet wrappers serving as ashtrays that littered the carpet where the girls were sprawled. 'Have you lost your mind? Don't you realise how dangerous smoking is?' she demanded, bending to scoop up the cigarette packet and a cheap lighter and rounding on Amanda. 'Are these yours? Take them — and get out!'

The sullen-faced girl snatched them from Kirsty's hand, then grabbed her school blazer from where it was draped over a chair back. As she sauntered from the room, she turned to Janey. 'See you tonight at the rink?'

'Definitely! I'll see you at — '

'Janey won't be going out tonight,' Kirsty interrupted coldly. 'And Amanda, please don't come to this house again. You're not welcome.'

'How *dare* you!' hissed Janey the instant her friend left. 'How dare you humiliate me like that!' She scrambled to her feet and glared at Kirsty, so furious she could scarcely speak. 'You've no right ordering me and my friends about. No right!'

'Janey — wait!' But the girl barged past her, pausing in the doorway.

'This isn't your house, Kirsty. And you're *not* my mother!' Janey snapped bitterly. She hadn't cried at the news of her parents' disappearance, but now tears of rage and resentment stung her eyes. 'We don't even want you here! Why don't you go back to London and leave us alone!'

* * *

The waterhole in the forest hollow was the first they'd come across since parting from Sam, Señor Bernaldez and Luis. Although they didn't dare risk drinking the brackish water, it was adequate for washing — just about.

'I'm not sure what I'm looking forward to most, Isobel,' remarked Angela wryly, wringing out her cotton shirt. 'Shampooing my hair, taking a proper bath in clean, hot water, or having a cup of freshly ground coffee. After this, I'll never grumble about facilities at the Castildoro hotel ever again!'

'At least we'll look clean and halfway decent when we arrive there,' said Isobel thoughtfully, using her fingers to tease the tangles from her wet hair. By unspoken agreement, during their days of walking from the wrecked plane, nobody had speculated upon the fate awaiting them when they reached Castildoro.

They'd become accustomed to the night skies being alive with military aircraft, but this morning they'd seen planes flying in daylight for the first time. And now they were close enough to the capital city to hear muffled explosions and bursts of gunfire. The agitated shrieking of monkeys high in the dense canopy of trees warned of yet more planes approaching. Despite the steamy heat, Isobel was suddenly cold.

Clambering from the shallows, she sat on the baked mud surrounding the waterhole. It was covered with the prints of animals — splayed reptilian claws, slender hooves, spiky bird-tracks and the large, flat paw-marks of wildcats. Isobel purposefully took an address book from her pocket and concentrated on carefully sketching the paw, claw and hoof prints. The notebook and pencil had been a Mother's Day gift from Janey and the boys. Isobel couldn't bear to part with it when she'd left the rest of her belongings behind on the plane.

'Are you keeping a diary?' asked Angela with interest, joining her on the bank.

She shook her head. 'It's a sort of letter for my children. I jot down how clear the stars are . . . describe the wonderfully coloured birds . . . how much like Robinson Crusoe Douglas looks now he can't shave . . . It's only silly, wee things but . . . ' Isobel smiled self-consciously, unable to put her feelings into words. 'Somehow, while I'm writing, it's like I'm talking to them.'

'You've two boys and a girl, haven't you?' Angela asked, offering Isobel the tin mug of paste she'd ground together from barks, leaves and tuberous roots. They'd used up their supply of insect repellent and, although this ancient Inca remedy had an unpleasantly sweet odour, it did soothe the burning, itching bites. 'I've seen pictures of the children and you in Douglas's tent at the dig. You have a beautiful family, Isobel.'

'I keep thinking about them expecting me home last Tuesday,' she responded sadly, a faraway expression in her eyes. 'Imagining them waiting and waiting, but I never came. They'll be feeling so lost and afraid.'

'It might be possible for us to make a telephone call when we get into town,' suggested the younger woman gently. 'Or mail a letter, at least.'

'What will it be like, Angela?' murmured Isobel. 'You know and understand this country. What'll happen to us?'

'My guess isn't any better than anybody else's.' She gave a resigned shrug and got to her feet. 'Political unrest can rumble on for years down here and then suddenly explode into open warfare. Often it's over as quickly as it erupted, and life goes on pretty much as before,' she continued as they clambered up the slope to rejoin Douglas and Karl. 'Despite the military activity, the situation in Castildoro might not be as bad as we fear. But whatever the situation, we do have to return,' she concluded practically. 'Because we've no place else to go.'

They were about an hour from the city limits, following a rutted track cut between forest and cane fields, when the horrendous roar of aircraft drew nearer and passed directly overhead. Isobel looked up, getting her first proper sighting of the planes. The pilots were flying low, the aircraft appearing curiously old-fashioned. Instinctively, she pushed her fingers into Douglas's clenched hand. He didn't turn to her. His face was raised, his eyes narrowed as he too watched the planes flying towards Castildoro. Isobel averted her eyes from the aircraft. If the city was about to be bombed, she didn't want to watch it.

'Must be more than a hundred . . . ' Karl broke off, hastily adjusting the lens on his binoculars. 'They're dropping parachutists!'

Douglas took the glasses.

'Not on the city, Karl — at the far side of it.'

Isobel turned back in time to see the great mass of planes disappearing beyond the distant saw-toothed foothills.

When they started walking again, they moved more cautiously than ever before. At a blind corner, Douglas edged on alone, threading through the trees.

'Track's blocked by a Jeep and a half-dozen soldiers,' he told Isobel and the others a few minutes later. 'There's no way we'll get by without being challenged. And they're heavily armed.'

Isobel moved closer to him and he put his arm about her shoulders. From the look in his eyes, she knew he was blaming himself yet again for bringing her to Castildoro. She raised her chin confidently, desperate to reassure him, determined not to let him sense how scared she was. 'Aren't there any other roads into the city?' she asked steadily. 'Smaller ones that might not be guarded?'

Douglas nodded. 'If Karl and I get onto that ridge . . . ' He shielded his eyes, pointing to the high ground above the rows and rows of tall sugar cane, ' . . . we can work our way down through the fields and get close enough to see exactly what's going on in the city. Then we'll know if we've a chance of reaching the hotel. I want you to stay here, Isobel.' He glanced quickly from her to Angela. 'Both of you. Sit tight, and keep well out of sight.'

'Where you go, I go,' responded Isobel quietly. 'We agreed not to be separated, Douglas.'

'It makes no sense for Isobel and me to hang around here,' chipped in Angela, using her shirt sleeve to rub away the perspiration trickling into her eyes. 'We could be picked up by the military at any time. Let's stick together and just get going.'

It was a hard climb to the ridge, with the midday sun beating relentlessly down. Isobel's legs were leaden, her heart thumping, as Douglas hauled her up the final yards. She found herself on a stony ledge, high over the cane fields, which offered a good view of Castildoro.

'Keep down,' warned Karl, inching forward to lie on his stomach. He propped his elbows on the ground and adjusted the binoculars before sweeping the ground below the ridge.

'What — ?' Angela began in a low voice, but Douglas instantly raised a forefinger to his lips. Following his gesture downwards, they saw a solitary soldier patrolling the field perimeter close to the machine store. No more than seventeen or eighteen years old, the boy was wearing the dull green battle clothes of General Ortega's army, and an automatic weapon was slung carelessly across his shoulder.

Wordlessly, the binoculars were passed from one to another. When Isobel's turn came, her hands were trembling so much that Douglas needed to steady the glasses for her. Controlling the panic rising within her, she stared down into Castildoro.

The streets were empty of people. No old men gathered beneath the shady awnings outside the cantina, dozing away the afternoon or playing checkers. No children were racing through the dusty streets or selling fruit and ice from the corners. No women drawing water from the communal pump in the square.

Instead, there were soldiers everywhere. They sauntered through the deserted streets and stood outside the bank, police station and post office. They were stationed behind barricades of sandbags high on the flat rooftops of the public and government buildings. And all of them looked as young as the boy in the cane field.

Isobel was anxious to get away from the ledge as quickly as possible, but when they were descending the ridge again, her chest became so constricted with fear she could scarcely breathe. She was terrified that the crack of a twig or rattle of a loose rock would alert the armed sentry in the cane field.

Not until they were safely across the guarded track and amongst the forest trees did any of them breathe easily. It was Angela who spoke first. 'We haven't a drop of fresh water left, and hardly any food. We can't get into Castildoro, so what do we do?'

'The dig,' said Karl simply. 'It's our only hope.'

'That's another six or seven hours of hard walking away,' Douglas commented, his eyes fleetingly upon Isobel.

'We could make it before nightfall,' argued Angela, looking to Isobel for support. 'The site's well equipped. We'll have food, water, vehicles. Radio — if we're lucky.'

'And if the rest of the team are still working there,' put in Karl. 'We'll be able to link up with them and make our plans accordingly.'

With the shock subsiding, Isobel felt

drained in mind as well as body. Angela and Karl were right, though. She met Douglas's anxious eyes and nodded positively. 'I think we ought to keep going and get to the dig.'

The sun was dipping gold and red at the horizon when Isobel and the others stumbled wearily into the site of the archaeological excavation. None of Douglas's team were there. It looked as though they hadn't been at the dig for some considerable time. Poles and ropes dividing the grids were flattened and strewn across the sandy ground, benches were overturned, and books, trays and discs tossed aside. Angela's old station-wagon and a Jeep were bogged down into the soft earth and abandoned.

In the gathering gloom of evening, the four wandered amongst the looted tents and huts, assessing what was left. 'Whoever did this was in a hurry. They only stole what they could easily carry — which makes us lucky,' Karl remarked ironically, emerging from one of the sheds. 'The radio and transmitter are still here.'

Suddenly, brilliant light flooded the darkness, pinning them in its dazzling beam. Isobel glimpsed the dull green of a military uniform behind the light and tried darting to Douglas's side. A harsh voice froze her where she stood.

'Don't move!' The command was chillingly quiet and very, very near. 'Any of you!'

★ ★ ★

'George, that was a fine sermon,' Paul Ashworth was saying to Reverend Wakefield as he and Kirsty shepherded the children from the village church after the Sunday service. 'I'm sorry one of us dropped a handful of marbles!'

'It's difficult being still when the sun's shining outside,' the elderly minister replied philosophically. 'Eh, Robbie?'

'Yes,' the small boy agreed readily,

tugging at Kirsty's dress. 'Can I ride my bike now?'

'Off you go!'

'Miss Carmichael, I understand from my daughter you're to stay on in Ferneys Beck?'

'For a while,' Kirsty confirmed with a smile.

'It goes without saying we're keeping your family in our prayers at this distressing time,' the minister continued. 'But if there's anything Kate or I can do, anything at all, please don't hesitate to ask.'

'That's very kind, Mr Wakefield,' she returned warmly. 'Actually, Kate's been a great help already.'

* * *

'What was that all about?' Paul asked curiously when they started down the wide path beneath the arching yews. 'I didn't realise you knew Kate Wakefield.'

'Got you guessing, hasn't it?' Kirsty chuckled. 'Thanks to Kate and Mrs

Bell, I'm off to Manchester tomorrow!'

'Ah yes, your audition,' murmured Paul reflectively, falling into step beside her as they passed through the high church gates.

Kirsty had been very young when he'd first met her at Isobel and Douglas's wedding. Romance hadn't exactly blossomed between bridesmaid and best man. Oh, in the years following they had seen each other occasionally at Christmases and christenings. Sometimes, they'd even gone out for lunch or dinner; but it wasn't until two summers ago their easy-going friendship had unexpectedly changed forever. Kirsty had turned up at Chimneys for one of her spur-of-the-moment holidays, and they'd found themselves spending almost every day and evening together. At some point Paul had fallen in love, confident Kirsty felt the same.

Then a call from her agent came — and within a couple of hours Kirsty was gone, just as suddenly as she had arrived. Now Paul drew a steadying breath, taken aback at how much it still hurt to remember Kirsty's rejection and their bitter quarrel. He glanced at her. She was laughing, carefree, waving wildly to Robbie as he and two little friends pedalled furiously around the green on their trikes.

'Do you think you'll get this role?' Paul asked rather brusquely.

'There's some as thinks ah will, chuck!' She grinned, slipping easily into the broad Lancashire accent she'd spent hours perfecting. 'If I don't, it certainly won't be for the want of trying — or wishing! I want it so badly, I — '

'Auntie Kirsty!' Robbie was wobbling by. 'Can Joe and Penny come to our picnic?'

'If their mums say it's OK,' replied Kirsty cheerfully. 'The more the merrier!'

'A picnic instead of traditional Sunday lunch was a good idea,' remarked Paul, gaining a grip on his wayward thoughts.

'Izzie always makes Sunday such a family occasion. I thought if I tried to do the same, it'd only make her absence all the worse for the children,' answered Kirsty solemnly. 'They're missing their mum and dad terribly, of course, and this is the first Sunday when Izzie ought to have been home from her holiday.'

'Paul! Kirsty!' hailed Kate Wakefield from the church gates, scurrying out along the lane after them. 'Robbie's glasses — I found them amongst the hymn books. He must've dropped them.'

'Thanks, Kate. He keeps leaving them all over the place.' Kirsty shook her head in light-hearted exasperation. 'I hadn't even noticed he wasn't wearing them.'

'Small children often take a while adjusting to wearing glasses,' Kate said, returning Kirsty's smile. 'By the way, bring Robbie to the parsonage as early as you like tomorrow. I have several little ones whose parents drop them off before going to work, so we open our doors at breakfast-time. I think it's unlucky to wish actors to break a leg, Kirsty,' she concluded warmly, 'but I do hope tomorrow's audition goes wonderfully and you get the part — that soap's one of my favourites!'

She strode off briskly, pausing at the church gates to glance over her shoulder to Paul. He was a tall man, his dark head inclined towards the much shorter Kirsty as they strolled side by side.

They were chatting amiably together, and she heard them laughing as Robbie pedalled precariously between them. As one, they each took hold of a handgrip, giving the trike a helpful pull over a bumpy patch on the path. Abruptly turning away, Kate hurried through the gates and up into the empty church.

★ ★ ★

Though it was long past midnight, Kirsty was wide awake. She'd lit a fire in the sitting-room and was stretched out along the window seat, studying her script. She already knew it by heart, but . . .

A gentle tapping and an unexpected face on the other side of the glass had her flying into the hall and pulling open the front door. 'Josh!' she exclaimed in astonishment, virtually falling into his outstretched arms. 'Oh, Josh! What are you doing here?'

'Soon as I finished at the studio, I hit the road! This is going to be an important day for you, sweetheart. I want to be a part of it.' He held her tightly for a moment, glancing around as Kirsty drew him indoors. 'Thought you might need some moral support, too.'

'Oh, people have been really helpful,' she replied enthusiastically, raising her face for another kiss. 'I can't believe you're really here!'

'Auntie Kirsty . . . ?' a thin, sleepy voice drifted down the stairs.

'That's Robbie — I'll have to see what he wants.' She grinned ruefully, moving out from Josh's embrace. 'Stay right where you are.'

But when Kirsty came downstairs again, Josh wasn't where she'd left him. He was in the kitchen, standing at the stove with his back toward her. He'd discarded his jacket and pushed his shirt-sleeves up over his forearms. There was a cardboard box on the table that hadn't been there earlier.

She paused in the doorway, watching him. Josh's movements had an easy economy, with none of the flashiness some men displayed when they were cooking and hoping to impress. He glanced around and smiled at her. 'Hi. I didn't hear you coming down.'

'I've been here a while.' She crossed the room, slipping her arms around his waist and resting her cheek between his shoulder blades. 'I like watching you cook.'

'That's because I'm doing all the work!' he laughed quietly.

Kirsty stood on tiptoe, touching her lips to his ear. 'No, it isn't. What are you making anyway?'

'Pasta, of course! I'm half-Italian. What else would I cook at two-thirty in the morning?'

'It smells great,' she remarked appreciatively. 'I hope it doesn't awaken the children and bring them downstairs.'

Josh stretched out a hand and closed the kitchen door firmly. 'Problem solved! I brought a few other things,' he went on, going over to the cardboard box. 'The wine's already open, and these are for you.'

'They're beautiful! Thank you so much!' She buried her face in the fragrant petals of the long-stemmed carnations, laughing as Josh darted back to the stove to rescue a bubbling pan. 'I'll set the sitting-room table. I'm sure Izzie has some fancy candles tucked away somewhere.'

After they'd eaten, they took their wine to the fireside rug. Kirsty curled up next to Josh, her head against his chest.

'After that long drive, you must be

exhausted,' she murmured at length. 'I'll fix up the spare room.'

'Don't bother.' He stretched contentedly. 'I'll be fine down here. But you should get some sleep.'

'Wouldn't be able to,' she said, nestling closer. 'Besides, I don't want to be away from you, even for a second!'

★　★　★

Early-morning sunshine was flooding the room when Kirsty opened her eyes. Josh's jacket was still draped over her and he was smiling down at her, offering a tall glass of orange juice.

'I let you sleep as long as possible, but . . . ' He shrugged apologetically.

'Oh, no!' She came wide awake with a jolt, elbowing herself up against the couch cushions. 'What time is it? What — '

'Take it easy! The housekeeper — Mrs Bell, isn't it? — came and sorted out the kids. They've gone, and so has she. Everything's under control.'

'Winifred's terrific,' sighed Kirsty thankfully, butterflies starting to flutter in her stomach as she thought ahead several hours to the audition that had the power to change the rest of her life. 'Josh, what do you think of my hair?'

'I love it.' He smoothed his fingertips through the soft waves, fanning them about her shoulders. 'I told you that last night.'

'Mmm, so you did.' She smiled, remembering. 'Actually, I meant for my character! Should I pin it up? Wear lots of colourful slides, maybe?'

'If it helps create the illusion, why not?' He followed her from the room, glancing at his watch as she sped up the stairs. 'Don't take too long, though. We have to set off soon.'

Josh was waiting in the hall with the front door open and Kirsty was racing downstairs when the telephone rang.

'We're already running late.' He grasped her wrist as she reached to answer it. 'Leave it!'

'Can't. Suppose it's Mum? Or Izzie, even?'

Josh agreed warily, knowing what Kirsty was like once she got on the phone. 'I'll put your bags in the car.'

'It was Kate Wakefield at the playschool,' Kirsty explained breathlessly some time later, sliding into the passenger seat. 'Robbie's had a bit of a scuffle with a bigger boy. Kate said neither one is hurt, but Robbie's upset. His nose has been bleeding.' She shook her head in disbelief. 'They're hardly more than toddlers, Josh.'

'It probably isn't nearly as alarming as it sounds,' he replied reassuringly, briefly touching her cheek before he started the car. 'Small boys do have fights sometimes. And nose bleeds, bruises and skinned knees.'

'Even so, Kate said Robbie was crying, wanting his mum.' Kirsty was subdued as they approached the village.

'Josh — stop! That's the parsonage over there. I'll just pop in and check

158

Robbie's OK.' Hastily unbuckling her seat-belt, she scrambled out. 'Won't be a minute.'

'I'll wait here.' Josh checked his watch. 'Be quick!'

Kirsty sprinted over the gravelled driveway and up the stone steps into the double-fronted Georgian parsonage. Pausing in the parquet hall, she tried to get her bearings.

'In here,' Kate Wakefield called cheerily from a colourfully decorated room to the left of the hall. 'We're playing a rhyming game.'

Kirsty whirled around, seeing Robbie tumbling from Kate's lap and making a beeline towards her. 'Auntie Kirsty!' He wasn't crying now, but his eyes were large and swollen, his flushed cheeks streaked with dried tears.

'What is it, darling?' she whispered, bending to pick him up. 'What's wrong?'

Robbie flung his chubby arms about her and Kirsty dropped to her knees, holding him tight.

'Auntie Kirsty,' he mumbled, burrowing his face into her neck, 'want to go home!'

'Shhh, it's all right,' she comforted him, scarcely recognising a sudden surge of unfamiliar tenderness as she cuddled him. 'I'm here.'

'Kirsty,' Josh's voice came from a few yards away in the parsonage doorway, 'we have to go-now!'

Robbie whimpered, clutching at her fearfully. Kirsty instinctively tightened her own grasp. 'He needs me, Josh,' she answered softly, wonderingly, without looking up. 'I can't go away and leave him. I just can't!'

6

'Kirsty, they won't give you another audition,' warned Josh in a low voice, watching her cuddling Robbie. 'It's now or never. You don't have any choice!'

'Yes, I do,' she answered simply. Beaming reassuringly at Robbie, she set him down in front of her, her hands lingering on his shoulders. 'Is there anything you need to bring home with you? Then off you go and fetch it.'

Robbie turned, taking half a dozen steps before stopping and trotting back to her. He curled his small fingers around hers anxiously. 'You won't go away?' the little boy implored earnestly, raising his face to hers. 'Please don't go away, Auntie Kirsty!'

'I won't go, Robbie. Promise,' she murmured, her voice catching. 'Now go and get your stuff.'

His feet thumped on the wooden

floor as he ran around the corner and out of sight. Kirsty turned to Josh.

Before she could speak, he began, 'I know this is upsetting for you, sweetheart, but we really *must* get a move on.'

Kirsty shook her head impatiently. 'Josh, I've told you — '

Pressing a forefinger to her lips, he silenced her protest. 'Listen to me. Robbie had a scrap with a playmate — and now it's over,' Josh said practically, conscious of the minutes ticking by and the long drive ahead through rush-hour traffic. 'Once we've gone, he'll settle down. In no time, he'll be racing around playing with his friends as if it never happened.'

'But you heard what Robbie said!' she exclaimed, her eyes wide and troubled. 'You saw how upset he was.'

'Think what you're doing,' he demanded urgently. 'You've worked and waited years for an opportunity like this audition. Don't let it slip away, Kirsty! You may never get another.'

'D'you think I don't realise that?' she cried, her eyes sparkling up at him. 'Kate Wakefield knows Robbie far better than I do, but it was me he asked for, Josh! It was me he ran to just now. I'm not going off and leaving him, not for anything in the world!'

'Fine. We'll take him with us,' declared Josh abruptly, his patience running low. Kirsty's heart tended to rule her head where her family was concerned. Somebody had to watch out for her interests. 'I can look after him while you're at the studios.'

'I'm not dragging him to Manchester and letting him hang around for hours while I audition!' she responded adamantly, flushing. 'He doesn't even know you, Josh. What Robbie needs is to go home. Now. With me. I'll just have a quick word with Kate.' Turning on her heel, she made for the playroom. 'I'll see you in the car.'

They hardly spoke during the drive back to Chimneys. 'All those years of hard work,' commented Josh tersely, catching her eye in the mirror as she sat in the rear seat with Robbie. 'I can't believe you've thrown it all away.'

'I haven't. There'll be other parts,' she replied positively, looking away so he couldn't read her doubts. 'Anyhow, it's done. I don't want to talk about it anymore.'

'Well, I do! I drove all night to — '

'I'm sorry you went to such trouble for nothing!' she snapped tartly. 'I didn't ask you to come to Yorkshire.'

'That isn't what I meant, and you know it!' he retorted, stung by her sharpness. 'I came up here because I know how important today was for you, Kirsty — which is more than any of your family appear to do!'

'Josh!' She glowered at him, casting a meaningful glance in Robbie's direction.

Josh inclined his head slightly. He was pale, and Kirsty knew he was seething. But for Robbie's presence, they'd be quarrelling violently about the impulsive decision that had probably changed the rest of her life.

★ ★ ★

Once home, Robbie took his toy train and a pocketful of biscuits and happily dashed across the garden to the tree-house.

'At least he's happy now,' Kirsty sighed aloud, standing in the empty kitchen. Less than an hour ago, she'd rushed from this house with such high hopes for her future. Now there was nothing. 'I'll telephone Manchester,' she remarked flatly, hearing Josh coming in through the back door, 'and tell them I'm not coming.'

'Afterwards,' Josh said as he strode into the kitchen, tossing his car keys on to the table. 'First, we have to talk. About you. About what's happening here.'

'Leave it, Josh. Please.' She shook her head wearily, switching on the kettle. 'You're angry — '

'You bet I'm angry — but not with

you!' he exploded impatiently. 'I'm angry *for* you, Kirsty. Your family is taking advantage of you. They're selfish and — '

'You've no right saying that!' She whirled around, her eyes flashing. 'You've never even *met* my family!'

'I love you. That gives me the right. Do you think I liked watching you choose between a child and your own future? You shouldn't have had to do it. Your mother ought to be here.'

'Mum can't be in two places at once,' retaliated Kirsty loyally. 'Dorrie needs her in Auchlanrick.'

'I'm sorry your sister's pregnant and unwell — but she's in hospital, getting the best possible care, and she has her husband at her side. There's no reason for your mother to stay up there.'

'Graham can't be with Dorrie all the time,' she mumbled, her hands trembling as she set the mugs on to a tray. 'He has a business to run, and Mum reckons he's having problems.'

'What about *your* business? Your

career? Or don't your problems count?' demanded Josh furiously. 'Now the crisis in Scotland is past, your mother could come back here. Instead, she's taking it for granted you'll put your life on hold — and sacrifice your career and your future.'

'I'm helping out, that's all,' muttered Kirsty. 'It's only temporary.'

'*Temporary* has a habit of drifting into permanent,' continued Josh relentlessly. 'Nobody knows when Isobel and Douglas will be home. Suppose they don't come home? Are you planning on staying in Yorkshire forever?'

Kirsty gasped, the tray almost falling from her unsteady hands. She set it down with a clatter, catching her lower lip between her teeth.

'I'm sorry!' Josh pulled her into his arms, holding her tightly against him. 'I came here to help you, not make you unhappy.'

'I — I *wanted* to stay with Robbie. But . . . ' She broke off dejectedly, only too aware of everything she'd given up.

'But I *am* scared about the future. I've already had to withdraw from that French sportswear commercial and a few other jobs. I've been independent since I was eighteen. I'm used to making my own decisions. Suddenly things are happening, and I'm not in control of my own life anymore. What's going to become of me, Josh?'

'I wish I could do something,' he murmured.

'You're here,' she whispered simply.

'It's ages since we've had a whole day together. Why don't we go up into the hills?' he suggested at length. 'Just the two — three — of us,' Josh amended with a grin, remembering Robbie. 'And this evening, I'll take you out for a romantic dinner.'

'The hills will be lovely,' she responded enthusiastically. Josh's smile always made *her* smile. 'But I can't go out tonight because — '

'Of the children!' he laughed, putting an arm about her shoulders. 'We'll stay in, then.'

'Janey's meeting Marcus at the movies and Alasdair's never any bother at all. Once Robbie's tucked up, we can have a quiet evening.' Kirsty's eyes were shining. 'I'll cook something nice. I'm pretty good, you know. What do you say?'

'Yes — on one condition,' he replied, gathering her to him again. '*I'll* do the cooking!'

*   *   *

He did. And while Josh was setting the table that evening, Kirsty went upstairs to check on Robbie.

'All that racing round in the hills did the trick.' She grinned at Josh, who was lighting the candles. 'Robbie was fast asleep as soon as his head touched the pillow.'

'It was a good day.' He glanced up. 'You weren't wearing that dress a few minutes ago!'

'Special occasion.' She leaned across the table to kiss him. 'I felt like dressing up.'

'Careful!' He shielded the candle flame with his hand. 'Besides, dinner's ready.'

Josh's grandparents and mother were restaurateurs, and although he hadn't joined the family business, Kirsty was convinced he could have become a top-class chef. 'This is absolutely wonderful,' she sighed blissfully, chinking her glass to his. 'The food, the music, and especially — '

The back door banged open and slammed shut. High heels clicked rapidly along the hall.

'That's Janey!' Kirsty was on her feet and out of the sitting-room in a flash. The teenager was at the foot of the stairs. Janey stared at her aunt for an instant before bursting into noisy tears. She didn't pull away when Kirsty put her arms about her.

'I waited and waited, but Marcus didn't come!' gulped Janey. 'And then — then — '

Josh tactfully made himself scarce while Kirsty helped the distraught girl upstairs to her room.

'How is she?' he enquired a little while later when Kirsty came down to make Janey a mug of hot chocolate with marshmallows.

'Inconsolable,' she replied bleakly. 'Marcus was her first boyfriend. He not only stood her up tonight, but Janey saw him in town with another girl.'

'Poor kid.' Josh grimaced sympathetically, pausing. 'Look, I think I'll slip away. I'd have to be leaving in an hour or so anyhow.'

Kirsty nodded, gazing sadly at the cold remnants of their lovely dinner. 'I'm sorry our evening was spoiled.'

He gave a resigned shrug and kissed her goodbye.

They'd said goodbyes before; faced lengthy separations before. But somehow this felt different. Kirsty clung to Josh's arm as she accompanied him to his car.

'I'm so sorry, Josh! It's all gone wrong today,' she blurted, leaning in through the car's open window to kiss him for the last time. 'But we'll sort something out. We'll find ways to be together. Won't we?'

She waved him out of sight, watching until the car's rear lights disappeared between the dark hedgerows before returning indoors. Taking two mugs of hot chocolate upstairs, she could hear Janey's sobbing, and suddenly realised her own eyes were wet. She hesitated on the landing, unsure if the prickling tears were for her young niece, or for herself and Josh.

* * *

'Between you and me, Sheelagh, I still lie awake worrying about her and the babies,' Ailsa confided to her friend as they walked back from the shops. 'But that said, Dorrie's been so much brighter since the hospital discharged her. Being back in her own home has made a big difference to her wellbeing.'

'Be sure to tell her I was asking about her,' said Sheelagh Kerr when they reached Ailsa's gate. 'And I'll bring that pattern book by this afternoon.'

'Thanks. We've made plenty of newborn things, but Dorrie's keen to get started on rompers and wee dresses.' Ailsa frowned slightly. 'Graham hasn't said anything, but he doesn't want Dorrie doing it. He doesn't like her making plans for after the twins are born.

'Myself, I think it's a good sign Dorrie is keeping busy.' Ailsa took her key from her handbag. 'It makes her happy and helps keep her spirits up. It's far better for her to be occupied and cheerful instead of fretting and fearing the worst.'

Ailsa had no sooner got indoors than she heard noises from the kitchen. 'Dorrie! Whatever are you doing down here?' She shook her head anxiously. 'You should be up in bed. You know fine well what the doctors said!'

'Please don't fuss,' returned Dorrie gently. 'I'm not an invalid, Mum. I just need to be careful. Graham's coming home for lunch today, and I want to make something special for him.'

'I'd have done that willingly. You only had to tell me what you wanted.'

'You do far too much.' Dorrie smiled ruefully. 'Looking after Graham and the house . . . Waiting on me hand and foot.'

'I'm happiest when I'm busy too, you know that.' Ailsa shepherded Dorrie from the kitchen. 'I'll take over now. You go and put your feet up. You'll be rushed off them once those twins arrive!'

'Come and talk to me, Mum,' began Dorrie soberly, going through to the front room and sitting down in one of the big fireside chairs. 'You know how you've just mentioned the babies? Well, Graham never does anymore. When I asked him about names — if he liked Tom and Lucy — he just nodded and changed the subject. I love Graham more than ever, but sometimes I don't think I know him any better now than when we first married.' She raised disturbed eyes to Ailsa. 'I never know what he's really feeling, Mum. Or what's going on inside his head.'

'It's only his way, pet,' Ailsa tried to reassure her. 'It doesn't mean anything's wrong. Graham's a bit like your dad was. He's not the sort to show his feelings.'

After Ailsa returned to the kitchen, Dorrie was restless to do something useful. Before her pregnancy started to go wrong, she'd always handled the office side of Graham's painting and decorating business. And since coming home, she'd frequently asked him to bring her the books so she could catch up on the paperwork. He'd always refused.

Opening the sideboard drawer, Dorrie started sorting through the bundles of letters, invoices and scraps of grimy paper. She was alarmed to find several unpaid bills and a letter of complaint from Chadwick's.

This wasn't like Graham! He was always so careful about paying bills promptly. And as for Chadwick's . . . Dorrie read their letter again with growing confusion.

Graham had been overjoyed when he'd won that contract to paint the canteen and decorate the offices of their factory in town. Chadwick's would be his first important customer, and if he did a good job for them it might lead to bigger and better things.

Yet now, Chadwick's were complaining! Dorrie thoughtfully rubbed her fingertips against her forehead. None of it made any sense.

'Mum!' She hurried into the kitchen, the letter and bills still in her hands. 'What's going on?'

Ailsa saw the papers and hurried to Dorrie's side, trying to guide her towards a chair. 'I'm sure it's nothing for you to get upset — '

'Stop it! You're doing *exactly* what Graham's been doing — shutting me out!' Dorrie's voice shook. 'I'm not a child, Mum. Tell me the truth. Is Graham in trouble?'

'Everything finished, Graham?' called Stuart Donaldson, pulling into the driveway of the newly refurbished cottage.

'Just about, Mr Donaldson.' Graham didn't stop loading the cans of paint into his van when the sporty saloon drew up alongside and parked. 'It's all ready for you to move in.'

'I'll take a look!' said Donaldson with a grin, disappearing through the low front door.

Graham glanced after him, his eyes lingering on the attractive cream-washed stone cottage. He and his elder brother, Jim, had been born in a similar cottage, but theirs had been a working croft with few comforts. Graham had seen his parents — both dead now — struggling to make a meagre living, and sworn he'd never live like that. He'd fought bitterly with Jim because of it.

Stuart Donaldson emerged cheerfully

from the cottage, pushing his hands into the pockets of his slacks. 'You've done a good job, Graham. It looks splendid. My fiancee's going to be delighted.'

'Aye, it's a fine wee house,' answered Graham stiffly, unable to suppress a surge of resentment. If only *he* could have bought Dorrie somewhere like this when they were first married! But they'd still been in their teens, and if Ailsa hadn't offered to share her home, they wouldn't have been able to get married at all. Besides, Dorrie wanted to live with her mother. She'd been upset at the notion of leaving Ailsa on her own. Graham was fond of Ailsa, but he never had felt comfortable living under her roof. He didn't like being beholden to anyone, and when he'd started up his own business, he'd been determined that one day he and Dorrie would have a house of their own.

But where had all his fancy ambitions got him? Graham grimaced in disgust.

Instead of prospering, he was getting sucked deeper and deeper into problems he couldn't see any way out of.

'Zoe won't be here until later — wedding dress fitting.' Stuart Donaldson laughed, still admiring the cottage. 'Would you like to join me in the pub for some lunch, Graham?'

'No, thanks, Mr Donaldson. I want to look in at home, then I've got to get straight into town,' he replied. 'I'm due at Chadwick's this afternoon.'

When he got home, Graham was nearly as surprised as Ailsa had been to find Dorrie up and about.

'Don't you start, too, Graham! You sound just like Mum did,' protested Dorrie mildly. 'I feel fine, really I do. And since this is the first lunch-time you've been able to get home for ages, I've baked your favourite pasties.'

'*You* made them?' he queried in concern. Although he had noticed she was looking better, there was no sense taking chances. 'You shouldn't go overdoing things.'

'I haven't!' she exclaimed in good-natured exasperation. 'Mum did most of the real work.'

'Where *is* Ailsa?' he asked, washing his hands at the kitchen sink.

'Gone to the WI.' She bent carefully to take the flaky golden-brown pasties from the oven.

'I'll do that!' insisted Graham hurriedly, taking the hot baking tray. 'They look great, but I haven't much time. I have to be on my way to Chadwick's by half-past.'

'Graham . . . I was looking through the books this morning. I saw all those unpaid bills, and the letter from Chadwick's.' She'd intended to leave it until evening when they'd have time to talk, but the words just came out. 'Why didn't you tell me things were going so wrong?'

'Och, it's not that bad,' he replied confidently. 'Some of my customers are late paying, so I'm short of cash to settle up my own bills. As for Chadwick's — well, maybe I have bitten off a bit more than I can chew. But it's nothing a few extra hours of solid graft won't put right.'

'You're hardly ever home as it is,' she murmured anxiously. He looked worn out.

'I'm not afraid of hard work, especially now I've something to work for. You and . . . ' He hesitated, gazing down at her. 'And our family.'

'Tom and Lucy,' she whispered, touching his cheek. 'Don't worry, love. Everything's going to be all right this time. I can't explain how I know, but I do.'

He nodded wordlessly. Dorrie sounded so certain that he feared for her anew. How would she cope if something *did* go wrong?

'I've been indoors so long. I'd love to go out in the sunshine and walk and walk and walk!' She smiled up at him. 'Up to the loch, and have a picnic like we did when we were courting!'

'There's no chance of doing that,' he said, returning her smile. 'But I suppose we could eat the pasties in the back garden.'

He was fetching the folding chairs from the shed when he heard a clatter in the kitchen and looked through the open window. 'Dorrie?'

'It's all right — just knocked over the tea caddy.'

'Give me a shout when dinner's ready and I'll come and carry everything out.'

'Thanks. I'll be glad when I can — Graham!' She caught a sharp breath, but her voice remained perfectly calm. 'Graham ... I think you'd better come ... '

★ ★ ★

Tom and Lucy were born early that evening. For a few precious moments, Dorrie and Graham were allowed to hold their babies before they were rushed to the special care unit.

'I can hardly believe it. They're so perfect,' murmured Dorrie contentedly, as Graham helped her snuggle down into bed in the quiet, private little room. 'And so tiny!'

'Did you see their shiny wee nails?'

Even Tom, the bigger and heavier twin, had fitted easily upon his palm, and Graham's large, rough hands had felt so huge and clumsy that he'd been scared of touching the curling little fingers and toes.

'The clothes we've knitted will be far too big,' Dorrie remarked drowsily, leaning her head against Graham as he sat beside her on the bed. 'But you can get especially small things for premature babies. Will you ask Mum about it?'

'Och, there'll be time enough for that tomorrow. You get some rest now,' he said quietly, patting her hand. 'The doctor said I was to pop along to the unit for a minute or two. Will you be all right on your own?'

'Mmm,' she sighed sleepily, turning her head on the pillow. 'Will you put their picture where I can see it?'

183

He propped the photograph of the babies on the bedside cabinet and left the room.

The instant the door closed behind him, Dorrie felt horribly alone. Wide awake and gripped by cold, overwhelming fear, she reached out and picked up the photograph. A dry sob escaped her throat as she gazed helplessly at the two crumpled little faces.

She wanted her babies. Wanted to hold them. Have them with her. But all she had was their photograph, and the desperate hope Tom and Lucy would be strong enough to survive their first critical hours of life.

★　★　★

'Doctor Blundell?'

The soldier — they could now see he was a sergeant — spoke in a questioning tone. 'Please step forward.'

As Douglas did as he was ordered, the light was tilted to shine full in his face. Instinctively he raised an arm to shield his eyes, and a dozen more soldiers emerged from the night, their automatic weapons menacingly levelled on the four men and women trapped in their circle.

'My men react quickly. I advise you not to do anything else that might be misunderstood.'

The sergeant waved his hand, and the soldiers melted like shadows into the dark forest. As he half-turned to focus his attention on his prisoners once more, Douglas caught his first clear glimpse of the man. 'Soler!'

'You never expected to see me again!' the sergeant remarked with a humourless laugh, indicating the large bark-thatched sorting shed that had once doubled as Douglas's office at the dig. 'Wait for me in there. Just Blundell!' he added sharply when the others made to follow.

Isobel was clinging to Douglas's arm. After a brief hesitation, Sergeant Soler nodded his permission for her to accompany her husband. 'How does he know you, Douglas?' she demanded frantically when they were alone in the relative safety of the shed. 'Who is he?'

'His name is Enrique Soler,' explained Douglas, surveying the sorting shed with its rows of floor-to-ceiling stacking shelves.

The results of almost a full year's excavation had been stored in here. Thankfully, little appeared to have been damaged or even disturbed. Nothing of obvious value to interest looters, he supposed. Automatically righting his overturned desk, Douglas picked up his chair and a bench and gathered together some scattered documents. His coal-oil lamp had fallen upon the plankboard floor, but amazingly the smoke-stained glass chimney wasn't even cracked.

'The Soler brothers were employed by the dig,' he went on matter-of-factly, taking a book of matches from his desk drawer and lighting the lamp. 'Enrique was my foreman.'

'Then he won't harm us, will he?' she insisted desperately, Douglas's methodical calmness only serving to heighten her own agitation. 'Not if he's your friend!'

'Do you remember the day after you arrived in Castildoro?' he asked quietly. 'When Angie and Karl told us camping equipment had been stolen from the site and several workers hadn't turned up? Enrique and his brothers were amongst them.'

'I remember.' She stared up at him. 'You said he was a decent man and you trusted him!'

'I know I did. But this country is at war with itself, Isobel. Even the closest of friends and brothers may find themselves on opposite sides. I liked and respected Enrique, but I was his employer. Nothing more. He's turned his back on everything; left his wife and children and his home; become a thief and a volunteer for Ortega's army.' Douglas met Isobel's eyes despairingly. 'Soler's a soldier now. There's no point hoping — '

Douglas broke off as the shed door

swung open. Soler strode inside, the heels of his well-polished boots jarring on the hollow plankboard. Past him, through the open doorway, the site appeared to be deserted.

'Where are Angie and Karl?' demanded Douglas anxiously. 'What have you done with them?'

Soler didn't answer. He sauntered between the couple and seated himself at Douglas's desk. 'Our situations are reversed now,' he remarked wryly. 'You mightn't be aware that the capital city has fallen. Castildoro is ours, Doctor Blundell. Soon the whole country will be ours.'

'What about my colleagues?' persisted Douglas, his fingers clenching around Isobel's hand. 'Where are Angie and Karl?'

'Nobody will get hurt, provided you co-operate,' Soler continued smoothly. 'Where are the others?'

'There are no others,' Douglas answered warily. 'Only us four.'

'Lying is pointless, Doctor Blundell.

We've found the wreckage of your plane. We *know* who was aboard!' Soler's palm slammed flat on the desk. 'Those three men are enemies of the state. I ask you the question again — where are they? Where is Luis Rosales?'

If Isobel had ever heard the name before, she was too frightened to remember. Douglas, however, realised immediately that the former president's only son being with them on Sam's plane made their situation even more dangerous. General Ortega would stop at nothing to capture the young man.

'We don't know where the others are!' Isobel cried out suddenly. 'We split up after the plane crashed. We don't know where they are!' She was speaking the truth, and that gave her words conviction.

Soler looked from Isobel to Douglas. 'It's my duty to take you back to Castildoro for further interrogation,' he commented finally. 'However, I am deeply in your debt, Doctor Blundell. After my brothers and I stole from you, you had the power to make our wives and children pay for what we had done, but you did not.' He rose, formally extending his hand. 'I have an obligation to help you. But I don't want to know where you are going or when you are leaving.'

'We need rest,' replied Douglas, cautiously accepting Soler's gesture of conciliation. 'And enough time to collect supplies and repair the station-wagon.'

'I will report that this site has been searched and neutralised. You should be safe here for a short while,' remarked Soler, starting for the door. 'But if another unit should discover you, I can do nothing. My debt to you is paid in full.'

'What about your men?' ventured Isobel fearfully. '*They* know we're here.'

Soler turned to look down at her. 'My men do as I tell them, Mrs Blundell. They'll say nothing. However, it might be prudent to construct a hiding place in case of emergency — if you understand my meaning?' He paused at the door, tapping the hollow-sounding plankboards with the sole of his boot. 'I supervised the laying of foundations for this sorting shed. A crawl-space could soon be dug out beneath the flooring. When I'm off duty, Doctor Blundell,' concluded the sergeant in a low voice before stepping out into the moonlight. 'I will return.'

★ ★ ★

Digging the hiding place became their priority. After only a few hours' sleep, Douglas and Karl started work later that night. Levering up a section of the plankboard, they enlarged the gap between floor and ground. Then they hammered in new beams for extra support, and to lessen the echoing hollowness which might arouse the suspicions of somebody walking over the hiding place.

During the days that followed, they

were meticulous about tidiness. Accidentally leaving something lying about might signal their presence if a military patrol passed by. They also avoided lighting fires for cooking, and pushed Angela's station-wagon out of sight so they could repair it.

'Lunch, Karl! Tomato soup — cold and straight from the can!' announced Angela, entering the radio hut where he spent every spare moment. He'd been a radio enthusiast since boyhood, and although this equipment had been damaged, Karl was convinced he'd be able to coax it into working order.

'How's it going?'

'Pretty promising.' He was pleased with his efforts. 'I picked up a radio ham and kept repeating a message. I'm not certain he even heard me, but it's a start.'

'Well done.' Angela set the soup bowl and a mug of coffee on the table beside him.

'Thank you.' Karl smiled up at her, lightly covering her hand with his own.

Angela dropped the plastic spoons, moving her hand aside as she bent to retrieve them. It appeared perfectly natural, but wasn't. And Karl realised it.

'Angela, can't we try?' he murmured.

'What good would it do?' she asked quietly. 'We've already discussed this, Karl.'

'We were virtual strangers then,' he persisted. 'Everything's different now.'

'The only thing that's changed is instead of being in New York, we're out in the middle of nowhere. We're colleagues and friends — can't you be content with that?' Pushing aside the green canvas blind, she glanced from the glassless window as an ageing pick-up truck chugged and bounced over the rough track. 'Here's Soler. Are you coming out to see him?'

Karl Fischer shook his head, turning back to the radio. 'I've nearly got this thing fixed. Better I stick at it.'

Isobel and Douglas were helping Enrique Soler unload a variety of cardboard boxes when Angela joined them. He'd brought medical supplies, provisions, bottled water, and a bundle of shapeless shirts, shorts and hats similar to those he himself was wearing. And most importantly, a replacement tyre.

'I noticed the station-wagon has a puncture,' he commented, reaching into the truck. 'Here's some petrol. It's in short supply right now.'

'This is tremendous, Enrique!' responded Douglas gratefully. 'I can't — '

He was interrupted by a high-pitched shriek from the radio hut and Karl's yell of triumph.

Even before the others had time to realise what was happening, Enrique Soler had snatched up the jack from his truck and was racing across the site, bursting into the cramped hut.

'I told you not to use the radio!'

'I don't take orders from you, Soler!' Karl leapt to his feet, confronting the younger, stronger man. 'A radio link with the outside world is our best chance — '

'I'm putting my life — the lives of my family — at risk by helping you!' retorted Soler savagely. 'Don't you realise what you've done?'

He slammed the jack down onto the radio in a single blow, smashing the vital equipment irreparably. Without another word, Enrique Soler strode from the hut and started up his truck. In a cloud of dust he swerved from the site and onto the rough track toward Castildoro.

Shocked and unnerved by his violence, Douglas and Karl decided they'd better leave at once, instead of in another day or two as previously planned. Haste made them less careful than usual, and it was purely from good fortune Angela heard approaching vehicles as she was filling her station-wagon with petrol. Edging through the bushes to see the track, she instantly tossed the can aside and raced back to the site where the others were packing up.

'Soler! He's coming back!' she warned breathlessly, her lungs bursting. 'In uniform. Not alone. Must be twenty or thirty — '

Grabbing both women by the arms, Douglas propelled them toward the sorting shed. There was nothing they could do about their belongings that lay in plain sight.

Inside the sorting shed, Karl raised the false section of plankboard. First Isobel and Angela, then Karl, and finally Douglas himself squeezed into the crawl-space. Crouching there in the blackness, they scarcely dared to breathe. They could see nothing. Only hear.

Engines. Footsteps. Voices.

Enrique Soler was speaking respectfully as he led his commanding officer directly towards their hiding place . . .

7

The two men paused outside the sorting shed, their voices carrying clearly through the glassless window. The superior officer was firing questions. Soler answered concisely, with obvious respect.

Isobel couldn't understand what was being said, except for the name 'Luis Rosales' several times. She was terrified, lying there in the darkness, not even knowing if Enrique Soler was betraying them.

'Karl's radio signals were picked up!' Angela whispered, her mouth pressed up to Isobel's ear. 'I think Soler's in trouble for not locating us earlier.' She strained to hear above the racket of a further hurried, violent search. 'But he hasn't turned us in — yet!'

The claustrophobic blackness of their cramped hiding space was overwhelming. Isobel bit her lip to stop herself crying out as Soler and his captain stood directly overhead, their boots sending grit showering through the plankboards.

The two men spoke rapidly. Isobel and the others lay still. Waiting. Listening.

'Soler's been ordered to take all the dig's records,' breathed Angela.

Minutes seemed like hours, until at last the captain strode out from the sorting shed. Engines started up. The search party was withdrawing. But Enrique Soler still lingered in the room above them.

'If ever we meet again, Doctor Blundell — ' His low voice was cold and void of emotion. ' — it will be as enemies. Remember that.' Then he, too, was gone.

They remained hidden until evening. Then, clinging to the shadows, they fled into the forest clearing where Angela's station-wagon was hidden. While Angela drove as fast as she dared, and everybody was talking loudly at once, Isobel's thoughts unexpectedly strayed to Soler. What would happen to Enrique if the military ever discovered he'd helped enemies of the state escape capture?

Sam had given Douglas instructions about the route he, Luis and Cesar Bernaldez intended taking to the border. Progress was steady, and surprisingly quickly Angela was skirting a little-used railroad track. A solitary figure emerged from the bushes. It was Sam.

After they'd greeted each other, Angela found herself gazing from the vehicle's open window to where she could just about discern Cesar Bernaldez slumped under the shelter of a stand of trees. He was alone. 'Where's Luis?' she demanded in alarm.

'Gone for food.' Sam jerked a thumb. 'We take it in turns.'

She pocketed her keys, jumping down and striding away from the station-wagon.

'Angela!' called Sam warningly.

'I'll be careful!'

She met Luis returning from the share-cropper's home, a rucksack of provisions slung across his shoulders.

'Angela! You're safe! I was sure — ' He broke off, halting awkwardly. Then he moved forward to embrace her tentatively. 'Thank God you're all right!'

'We very nearly weren't. I'll explain later. What about you?' She searched his unshaven face. Luis looked so much older; unkempt, shabby. Just another itinerant labourer seeking work. 'Are you OK?'

'I am. But what word is there of my father?' he murmured urgently. 'The only newspapers we've seen are days old and filled with Ortega's propaganda. Did the military capture Papa? Do you know what's happened to him? Does . . . does he still live?'

'Yes, he's safe,' she answered simply. 'We never actually went back into Castildoro, but I was told your father and his government left before Ortega seized the city. They went into exile.'

Luis expelled a heavy breath, bowing his head. 'It's civil war,' he went on after a moment. 'There are still some men loyal to my father who are opposing Ortega. They're defending democracy. My country is fighting for its very life, Angela!' He looked away from her as they walked, frustrated and deeply ashamed. 'Yet I do nothing to help! I hide behind a brave and loyal old man, pretending to be someone I'm not!'

'Getting killed or taken prisoner wouldn't help your country,' responded Angela briskly. 'Your chance to serve will come. And when it does, you'll be as brave as any fighter.'

'I wonder about that,' he said frankly. 'I watch the planes, hear the gunfire, and I wonder.'

They continued in total silence until the rusted railroad tracks came into view.

'Did you see Cesar?' asked Luis, glancing at her sidelong. 'How do you think he looks?'

'Tired,' she replied guardedly, not wanting Luis to sense how deeply shocked she'd been at the deterioration in the elderly man's appearance. 'Travelling in the station-wagon, the remainder of the journey will be much easier for him.'

'It's too late.'

She saw Luis was crying, making no attempt to conceal the tears spilling from his dark eyes. 'Cesar is dying!'

$\star \quad \star \quad \star$

Following the railroad line drew them deeper into remote country. Whole days slipped past without their seeing a single other person. Running out of fuel was a constant worry. Everyone was all too keenly aware Cesar Bernaldez was no longer capable of proceeding on foot.

'Noguera grew up around the mine,' Sam told them when the isolated town lay just a short distance ahead. 'When the mine played out, Noguera pretty much closed down with it. But trains still pass through.'

Spreading the map across the bonnet of the station-wagon, he traced the railroad track. 'See, after Noguera, it snakes into all these one-horse towns and villages in the mountains and goes within a mile of the border at Gaviria. That's where we'll be crossing over.'

'Sounds easy,' remarked Douglas drily.

'All we need do is get off the train at the right time and — ' Sam retorted abruptly, breaking off when he saw Isobel's apprehensive expression. 'Don't worry, there's no checkpoint or guards. Not even a marker to show where this country ends and the next begins. Once we board that train, you're practically on your way home to Yorkshire.'

Clean-shaven and wearing a newly acquired second-hand work shirt and blue jeans, Luis was elected to go into Noguera to find out when the next train was due. He was pulling on his rucksack when Angela decided to go with him, but when she hurried over to collect her own rucksack, Isobel followed her.

'Do you think this is wise?' she enquired mildly.

'What could be more innocent than a couple of students trying to get away from the fighting?'

'That isn't what I meant,' pressed on Isobel uncomfortably. 'I don't want to interfere, but . . . well, perhaps you're not aware of it, but Karl is concerned you're spending too much time with Luis.'

Angela gave a long-suffering sigh and looked directly at the older woman. 'When I arrived in New York, Karl had recently been divorced. We were both lonely and at a loose end, and we went out a few times. That's all there was between us — and that's all there'll ever be.' Hitching the rucksack buckles more securely, she went on: 'But you're right about one thing, Isobel — It isn't any of your business.'

Angela and Luis were sweltering and dust-streaked when they reached Noguera shortly after noon. To their relief, the little town showed no sign of military presence. But when they got to the station, the ticket window was boarded up. An elderly man seated at the far end of the paint-peeled platform was watching them curiously.

'Three, maybe four trains come through a month.' He nodded amiably in response to Luis's enquiry. 'A train'll stop for water and coal, mostly — Noguera doesn't get many folk coming and going these days. Anyhow, you've just missed it. Won't be another till next week. 'Course, if you and the young lady *really* want a train ... ' His weathered features creased into a broken-toothed grin, and he pointed away beyond the clapboard station. ' . . . there's a fine one out there. Get up a head of steam, and away you go!'

'What?' Luis wasn't sure if the old

man was joking with him.

'It was carrying resistance fighters. Ortega's men attacked it.' The elderly man's eyes became grave. 'They took their prisoners and left the train standing out there on the spur.'

Luis found it exactly as the old man described. The antique steam locomotive stood, bullet-scarred and abandoned, a few miles west of Noguera.

★　★　★

'Far too slow and awkward to be useful to Ortega's troops,' commented Sam with satisfaction some hours later, jumping down from the engine after a cursory inspection. 'But she's still got plenty of coal and water aboard, providing you two are willing to bend your backs and get your hands dirty.' He glanced wryly at Douglas and Karl. 'We can be on our way to the border by morning.'

Despite Sam's confident prediction,

it was more than another twenty-four hours before the train was ready to move. By then, knots of townsfolk were surrounding it, sitting on the ground in orderly groups with bundles of weaving, boxes of produce, sacks of cacao and strings of tobacco.

'Let them on. There'll be an almighty commotion if you don't.' Sam brusquely swept aside Douglas and Karl's reservations. 'The last thing we need is to antagonise the locals. In fact, it's not a bad idea for us to take on passengers all along the line. Why not? A train packed with folk taking goods to market will be a lot less conspicuous than a train carrying half a dozen Europeans and Americans.'

★ ★ ★

The rattling carriages were crammed to bursting by the time the mountains of Gaviria slid into sight almost a week later. Sam had been driving since dawn, and Isobel manoeuvred through the crowded, lurching train with a flask of fresh coffee.

'Thank you, Isobel.' Flexing the stiffness from his muscles, Sam gestured to the flask. 'Will you keep me company? It gets pretty lonely up here.'

She smiled, pouring the coffee. 'All right.'

'How's Cesar?' asked Sam after a minute.

'Resting in the guard's van. We've made him as comfortable as possible,' she answered sadly. 'At least Luis is with him.'

Sam nodded. Isobel didn't need to say more. She stood next to him, sipping the hot, bitter coffee and not looking at anything in particular. The railroad was winding between the mountains, the sides of the ravine narrow and rising steeply with patches of florid poppies, clumps of spearthorn and trees that reminded her of stunted Scots pine.

'Legend has it that a mighty god lives inside these mountains. The ravine's echo is his voice,' commented Sam. He'd taken his eyes from the track only briefly, but now he turned back, dragging on the brake as the train rattled around a curve. The locked wheels screeched, spitting sparks.

Sam's gaze was riveted on the fallen tree sprawled across the line. Isobel was staring too, never doubting he would stop the train in time. She never knew what made her glance upwards at that precise moment, but what she saw terrified her. Motionless against the cornflower-blue sky was a ragged line of troops.

Isobel gasped Sam's name as the line began to move. Firing warning shots, a barrage of soldiers came pouring down into the ravine.

★　★　★

'I passed Janey in the lane,' remarked Winifred Bell, letting herself into Chimneys. 'Still moping like she's lost a florin and found a farthing, is she?'

'She really cared for Marcus,' sighed Kirsty. 'Losing him will hurt more than physical pain.'

'That sounds like the voice of experience,' commented Winifred, hanging up her cardigan. 'Or am I being too nosey?'

'Nope. You're right on it, as usual.' Kirsty smiled forlornly, leading the way into the kitchen. 'Fancy a cuppa and a slice of chocolate cake? I've just finished the icing. Kate Wakefield's popping in for a chat about Robbie at eleven o'clock. He seems to like her a lot at playschool, so it's a sensible idea we meet up. Paul Ashworth is coming along, too. Not only is he Robbie's godfather, of course, but the pair are very close, and Paul's really good with him.' She paused, surveying the cake sceptically. 'Kate is so capable at everything, I felt I had to make an effort and bake something fancy.'

'It looks grand, I must say. Very tempting,' declared Winifred, admiring the rich chocolate cake with its hazelnut paste filling and glistening coffee frosting. 'But it's so rich, I really shouldn't.'

'Neither should I,' opined Kirsty, cutting two extremely generous slices and pouring the tea. 'Missing that audition changed things between Josh and me, Winifred.'

'Bound to have done. You've not seen each other since neither, have you?' She spooned sugar into her teacup. 'Letters and phone calls are all well and good, but it's easy to get the wrong end of the stick when folk aren't face to face.'

'It's far more than that. We're drifting apart, I can feel it,' Kirsty confided unhappily. 'Josh is working at the recording company's studios near Paris. It was arranged ages ago, and he's rented a flat in Montmartre. I could have gone with him. My part in his life is getting smaller and smaller.' She paused, gazing unseeing at the willow-patterned dishes on the dresser. 'How long can I expect him to wait?'

'It hasn't been that long,' reasoned Winifred, 'even if it seems like it.'

'It's not because I don't trust him — I do. But I just can't help . . . worrying,' went on Kirsty, absorbed in her tangled thoughts. 'We're hundreds of miles apart with no prospect of being reunited, and Josh is alone. What if he finds somebody else?'

★ ★ ★

Kate Wakefield arrived punctually, and Kirsty showed her into the sitting-room, leaving her to chat with Paul while she fetched a tray of coffee and cake.

'Since the fight, Robbie hasn't wanted to go to playschool,' explained Kirsty when the three were settled. 'He gets upset, so I haven't pushed him. He starts proper school in September, so I don't want to risk putting him off.'

'I appreciate your concern, but I honestly don't think keeping him at home is the answer,' Kate returned sympathetically, glancing briefly at Paul, whose full attention was still focussed upon Kirsty. 'Playschool is a rehearsal for the children. Socialising and learning to cope with ups and downs is valuable experience for when they start school.'

'Robbie won't always have the option of staying at home whenever he has a problem,' observed Paul, looking steadily at Kirsty. 'I'm sure Kate will make certain there's no more bullying.'

'You can rest assured about that,' she confirmed immediately.

Kirsty hesitated, wondering what would be best for Robbie. If only Isobel was . . . No, there was no point thinking that. 'I expect you're both right,' she replied with a slight frown. 'I'll bring him in tomorrow.'

★ ★ ★

The following morning was gloriously summery. The instant she got up, Kirsty went around Chimneys flinging wide the windows and doors. Janey and Robbie were still asleep, but Alasdair

213

must have crept from the house at the crack of dawn to go bird watching. Kirsty was well into her daily exercise routine in the garden when she spotted him coming back along the beck. He waved and went indoors, then came running out again.

'Robbie's not in bed!' he shouted. 'His duffel-bag and panda are gone. I think he's run away, Auntie Kirsty!'

'Oh, no!' She rubbed her hand across her forehead, scanning the rambling garden, the fast-flowing beck and the woods beyond. 'You look around out here. I'll check the house!'

Alasdair nodded, racing across the grass. 'I'll shout if I find him!'

Having started in the attics and worked downwards, Kirsty was in the hall when Winifred arrived. Together they searched the large, cluttered cellars where there were so many nooks and crannies for a small child to hide.

'He's not here,' muttered Winifred at last, hands planted on her hips.

'What if — ' began Kirsty, breaking

off when she heard heavy footfalls along the hall above them.

'Kirsty! Alasdair's just told me there's still no sign of Robbie,' Paul shouted down through the cellar doorway. 'How on earth did he disappear from the house at this hour?'

'I was in the garden,' she answered distractedly, hurrying up the steep steps to join Paul in the hall, her imagination churning. Where could Robbie be? Suppose he'd tried to cross the beck, or wandered off on to the moors? If anything happened to him . . .

'And you didn't even notice he'd gone?' challenged Paul sharply, catching her arm. 'How could you be so irresponsible?'

'I don't need you blaming me. I'm already blaming myself!' she cut in, her eyes bright. 'If you can't do anything more useful than — '

'That's Alasdair!'

Kirsty was off and running from the house even as Paul heard the second shout.

'Robbie's under the bridge!' Alasdair pointed to the sturdy little stone bridge crossing the beck at the foot of Chimneys' garden. 'He won't come out!'

'I'll see to him. Thanks, Alasdair, you've done great!' Kirsty laughed with sheer relief. 'Go in and have some breakfast. You've earned it!'

Scrambling on hands and knees down the muddy bank, Kirsty peered under the arching lichen-covered stones. Robbie's big eyes stared back at her. 'So you're running away, eh?' she asked calmly, squeezing in to sit cross-legged beside him. 'I wish you'd told me what you were planning. We got a big fright when you weren't in bed.'

Robbie sniffed loudly but didn't say anything.

'Is it because of playschool?' she prompted after a minute, not looking at him. 'In case you get teased again about your new glasses?'

'They'll all laugh at me, and Jason'll hit me if I go back,' mumbled Robbie finally, fidgeting with his duffel-bag.

'Kate wouldn't let anybody tease you or hurt you again,' she reassured him. 'You know she wouldn't.'

'He'll punch me when she's not looking. That's what he did before.'

'Suppose . . . suppose you stay at home a bit longer?' suggested Kirsty slowly. 'You and I can draw and read exactly as you would at playschool, so when you feel ready to go back, you won't have missed anything. Would you like that, Robbie?'

He nodded, scrubbing a grimy little fist across his tear-stained face.

'Great!' She eased the duffel-bag from his side and wriggled out from beneath the bridge, reaching back for Robbie's hand. 'Out you come! I'll give you a start of five, then race you in to breakfast!'

With all his problems magically solved and his panda clutched tight in his arms, the little boy happily dashed away from the bridge and up towards Chimneys. Kirsty didn't follow at once, though, because Paul was standing alongside the beck, glaring at her.

'You should have been firmer, Kirsty,' he reproved. 'This little escapade could easily have ended in disaster.'

'You think I don't realise that? Robbie is four years old, Paul. He's missing his mum and dad, and being teased and bullied because he's started wearing glasses,' she retaliated hotly. 'Running away was his cry for help. People don't always use words to say they're unhappy and ask for what they need, you know.'

'You overreacted, giving in to him like that. Why must you always be so emotional? You're always rushing headlong into situations without a thought for the consequences,' he persisted rationally. 'The three of us agreed on the wisest way to tackle Robbie's difficulties. You've completely disregarded that. From now on, he'll assume whenever — '

'All right, all right, so I'm not an expert like Kate. And I don't know the children as well as you and she do. But they're in *my* care, and I'm doing what I'd do if they were my own children. If you — or Kate Wakefield — have a problem with that,' finished Kirsty, starting swiftly from the beck and away from him, 'it's just too bad!'

★ ★ ★

That afternoon, she was at one end of the kitchen table scribbling a letter while Winifred sat at the other, polishing brasses.

'Want me to post that on my way home?' Winifed asked.

'No, thanks. To tell the truth, I don't actually want to send it at all. It's to Gwen, my flatmate.' She leaned back in her chair. 'I'm giving up my room. I can't afford to go on paying my share of the rent.'

'I hadn't thought about that,' remarked Winifred, pausing in her polishing. 'But it must be right hard for you, what with not working and having no money coming in.'

'I've hung on to the flat as long as possible.' Kirsty shrugged, folding the notepaper into an envelope. 'But as Paul has pointed out several times, it's pointless keeping a place in London now I'm living here.'

'Once he'd told us about that radio message saying Doctor and Mrs Blundell were safe, I thought they'd be home and back with us in no time.' Winifred rubbed a horse brass vigorously.

'I did, too. But like Paul and Alasdair keep on telling us, it's a big country,' reflected Kirsty sadly, pausing for a moment. 'And a troubled one. All the civilian airports and telephone links are closed. Paul reckons it could be months before Izzie and Douglas can get out. He's keeping up pressure on the Foreign Office to find — '

'I'll get it!' Winifred rose at an impatient rapping at the front door. 'Probably the Scouts for old papers.'

She returned laden with flowers.

'Wasn't the Boy Scouts,' chuckled Winifred, setting the lavishly arranged floral basket onto the table before a speechless Kirsty. 'Don't just sit there gawping — open the card! What does he say?'

Kirsty did as she was told. 'They're from Josh,' she whispered, her eyes soft. 'He has a few days off. He's coming here, so we can be together!'

'There!' Winifred was pleased. 'Things'll work out, you'll see.'

'Hope so,' murmured Kirsty, squeezing the elderly woman's shoulders. 'Is that the time? I'd better go and get changed!'

In less than ten minutes she was downstairs again, wearing a swimsuit and carrying a bundle of fluffy towels.

'Hello, Kirsty.'

'Paul.' She greeted him warily. 'I thought I heard voices down here.'

'Seeing as how you two were fighting like cat and dog this morning,' commented Winifred, gathering up the cloths, 'I'd best make myself scarce and go and polish the door-knocker.'

'I want to apologise,' began Paul as soon as they were alone. 'For blaming — '

'I bit your head off, too,' Kirsty interrupted mildly, smiling. 'We were both scared and anxious. Let's just forget it.'

'No. I shouldn't have criticised you as I did,' persisted Paul seriously. 'You're doing a wonderful job with the children.'

'I couldn't manage without Winifred's help, or yours. You've been incredible,' she responded impulsively. 'Not only with the children, but with all . . . all the official stuff,' Kirsty faltered, suddenly aware he was studying her intently. 'I — er — I promised the boys a swim in the beck before tea. I can find a pair of Douglas's trunks for you, if you'd like to join us?'

'I'm en route to a meeting in Leeds,' replied Paul regretfully. 'But I'll collect you tomorrow, about one o'clock, for Janey's school sports' day?'

'OK.' She was still conscious of his gaze upon her. 'See you then!'

'Yes.'

However, Paul continued watching her as she walked down the garden to the beck. He didn't even look around when Winifred came into the kitchen behind him.

'Living here at Chimneys has changed Kirsty,' he said softly. 'Settled her down.'

'Her heart's still in London,' commented Winifred bluntly.

'That Josh character?' he queried disparagingly. 'It's not serious. How can it be? She's only known him five minutes.'

'And I've known you since you were in short trousers, Paul Ashworth. I don't want to see you get hurt again.' Winifred's brow knitted. 'Take my advice — forget any ideas of getting Kirsty back.'

'I can't. She's the only woman I've ever asked to marry me.' Paul glanced around from the window to meet

Winfred's eyes steadily. 'I still love her.'

* * *

'All set?' enquired Graham with a cautious smile, peering around the door.

Dorrie looked up from the open suitcase and glanced about the hospital room. Her belongings had been packed. The twins' pictures were safely in her handbag.

'I don't want to go home and leave Tom and Lucy, Graham! What if they need me and I'm not here?'

He swung the suitcase from the bed and took Dorrie's arm, leading her out into the corridor. He never knew what to say when she talked like this.

'I want to see the twins just once more,' she murmured, holding back as they made for the lift, 'to say goodbye and tell them I love them.'

'You've already said it a dozen times. The last time they were both fast asleep,' reasoned Graham, not releasing his hold on her arm. He knew fine well leaving Tom and Lucy behind in hospital must be awful for Dorrie, but it had to be done. He pressed the lift's call button. 'Come on, let's just go. It's best.'

Dorrie seemed about to comply, then froze. 'Do you hear that?' she exclaimed, her eyes wide. 'It's Tom crying!'

'It can't be.'

She shook free of Graham's grasp, hurrying from the lift and back around the corridor to the special care unit. Graham went after her, his heart sinking when he saw her standing with outstretched palms flat against the large plate-glass windows of the unit. She was trembling as she gazed down at her babies.

'Both still asleep!' Graham gently pulled her away. 'Come home, love.'

'You'll bring me back to see them tomorrow?'

'Of course,' he promised. 'I'll finish work early tomorrow night and — '

'No! First thing in the morning. I want to be here when Tom and Lucy wake up.'

'Dorrie, you need rest,' he began. 'And I daren't take any more days off.'

'Then I'll come on the bus.' She cast a backward glance to the unit.

'All right,' he relented, because he couldn't think of anything else to say. Perhaps Ailsa could persuade Dorrie to see sense. Women were better at handling this sort of thing. 'I'll bring you on my way to Chadwick's. Just for tomorrow, mind.'

However, Dorrie continued her vigil each and every day after that. She was often alone, because she usually declined Ailsa's offers of company, and Graham was far too busy to spare the time.

* * *

Sunlight was streaming into their small kitchen one evening when they were having their meal. It was only the

226

fourth occasion they'd eaten together since Dorrie had been discharged from hospital. Graham watched, dismayed, as she listlessly pushed food around her plate, not touching a bite.

'Why don't you visit the Kerrs?' he suggested. 'Sheelagh's always asking you over.'

'I'd rather not, not yet. I've filled some rolls to take with you, and there's cold pie for when you get home from Chadwick's.' Dorrie left the dishes on the drainer and fetched a plastic box from the fridge. 'Will you be very late again?'

'Aye, don't wait up.'

Provided he pressed on, there was a slim chance he'd finish the Chadwick's job on time, which meant he'd avoid the hefty penalty written into the contract. Thoughtfully, he took the box of rolls Dorrie was holding.

'Shall I walk you over to the hall? Ailsa and the others would be glad of an extra pair of hands. It'd be better than you sitting here on your own.'

'I don't want to go out in case the hospital rings,' she replied simply. 'I'm happy to stay here and finish my sewing.'

Instead of driving straight to Chadwick's, Graham stopped off at the village hall. Ailsa was busy with last-minute preparations for the bring-and-buy sale.

'All this waiting and watching Dorrie's doing at the hospital — and her scarcely setting foot outside the house in case the doctors phone her — it's got to stop!' he declared agitatedly, keeping his voice low in the crowded hall. 'It's not right, Ailsa. I thought you would've talked to her; made her see sense!'

'Sense?' Ailsa bit her tongue, reminding herself Graham was very young and under a lot of pressure.

'Dorrie's heart and mind will be at that hospital until her babies are home where they belong,' she continued evenly. 'She's sure her being with Tom and Lucy helps them — and she's probably right. Any mother would feel the same.'

★ ★ ★

The house was in complete darkness when he got in late that night. In spite of his worries, Graham fell into a heavy, dreamless sleep the instant his head touched the pillow.

He wasn't certain what wakened him an hour or so later. Weary and disorientated, it was a while before he realised Dorrie wasn't beside him. What if there'd been a phone call — ?

Stumbling from bed, he went out onto the landing. No lights. Everywhere quiet. Then he noticed that the door at the end of the landing was ajar.

Dorrie was sitting in the darkness of the empty nursery, her head bowed, her hands folded. The cot quilt she'd embroidered for the twins was spread across her knees.

'For pity's sake, Dorrie!' Seeing her like this made something inside him snap. 'It's the middle of the night! What do you think you're doing?'

'Just sitting,' she replied sorrowfully, perplexed at his tone. 'Since I've had my own babies, I think about Izzie all the more. Being separated from your children is a terrible thing.'

'This is — ' Graham shook his head despairingly. Words failed him. 'Carrying on like this isn't going to help anybody. Not you, and not the twins!'

'You don't understand! You're never here!' she cried accusingly, getting up and turning her back on him. 'You hardly ever visit Tom and Lucy. Tom's getting stronger each day, but Lucy's still so tiny! You've no idea what it's like to watch her — she depends on that machine to even breathe!' Dorrie's voice was rising. 'Every time I leave her, I think I might never see her again. You just don't understand, Graham,' she repeated softly. 'You don't know what it's like, losing a baby.'

'Don't I?'

'It's not the same!' she cried,

shivering despite the warmth of the summer night. 'It's — it's different!'

'Aye, maybe it is.' Graham's words were scarcely audible as he forced himself to speak — for the very first time since Dorrie's miscarriage — of the child they'd lost before. 'But he was my son, too.'

★ ★ ★

He'd been at Chadwick's since before five that morning. As Graham drove home for an early lunch, he was preoccupied with calculating the amount of work still to be done. Turning into the drive, he hardly noticed Ailsa scurrying from the house.

'Can't stop. I'm off for the bus!'

He nodded absently, switching off the engine and going indoors. Dorrie was in the living-room, sitting at the table checking through the account books.

'How are the twins?' Graham asked at once. 'Is everything still all right?'

'Lucy'd put on a wee bit of weight when Nurse Petrie weighed her. Otherwise she's about the same.' Dorrie smiled wistfully up at him. 'But Tom really beamed at me today! I told him we were bringing him home this afternoon, and I'm sure he understood!'

Graham shut his eyes tightly for a few seconds. When he opened them again, he bent to kiss Dorrie's forehead before sinking heavily into one of the armchairs. 'I'll collect you in plenty of time for us to get over to the hospital. It's four-thirty, isn't it?'

'Yes. And we've had a cheque from Mr and Mrs Cronin.' Dorrie sorted through the papers set out into neat stacks on the table before her. 'For the work you did on their bathroom and kitchen.'

'About time they coughed up.'

'This came in the post, too.' She fingered several typewritten sheets. 'It's from the finance company. If you don't clear the arrears and bring your account up to date within seven days, they're going to repossess the van.'

Graham stared at the documents but made no attempt to take them from her. 'This is the last straw.' He expelled a resigned breath. 'I've been worrying about it for months, and now it's finally happened. I haven't the money to pay them, Dorrie.'

'There's the Cronins' cheque.'

'Nothing like enough,' he returned despondently. 'Without the van, I can't work. It's best if I pack up the business now and start looking for a job before I get any deeper into debt.'

'But you've always wanted your own business and you've already worked so hard — you can't give it up now, love!' she exclaimed, aghast. 'We'll make economies. Manage, somehow.'

'It's no use.' He faced her reluctantly. 'I'm sorry. I wanted so much for us — had such grand plans — but they've come to nothing, and all I've done is let you down.'

'Don't think like that!' she cried

fiercely. 'You've worked as hard as anybody could — and you *haven't* let me down! But you'll be letting yourself down if you sit around feeling sorry and talking about giving up. What about Chadwick's? Once they pay you, things'll start looking up.'

'Even though I've been putting in extra hours, there's no way I'll finish on time. It's too much work for one man,' he said dismally. 'And I certainly can't afford to hire somebody to help out.'

'No, but . . . ' Dorrie hesitated as an idea came to her. 'What about Jim?' she suggested in a rush. 'Perhaps he'll lend you a hand at Chadwick's.'

'Jim?' echoed Graham in disbelief at the mention of his elder brother's name. 'We've not seen him since Mother's funeral! Jim wouldn't give me the time of day — and I wouldn't ask him!'

'Don't be so hasty,' she argued in exasperation. 'You haven't talked to him in years. How do you know what he'd do? You're fighting to save your livelihood; our family's future. Surely it wouldn't do any harm to get in touch with him?' persisted Dorrie. 'After all, you and he are brothers.'

'You don't realise what you're saying. He and I were never close, not like you and your sisters.' Graham got up, pacing the room. 'You don't know the bitterness between us. I'd rather lose everything than go cap in hand begging Jim for a favour!'

8

'I don't see you have any choice!' exclaimed Dorrie, stung by her husband's anger and stubbornness. 'Your brother surely won't hold a grudge over something that happened when you were seventeen.'

'I walked out when my family was in trouble,' Graham muttered, glowering at her. 'I can't — won't — ask Jim for help now because I'm in the same boat they were then.'

'But you'll end up in court if you don't find some money to pay off your debts! And you won't be able to finish the Chadwick's job on time without an extra pair of hands helping with the work.' Dorrie broke off as the cooker timer buzzed. 'We have Tom and Lucy and their future to think about now, Graham,' she concluded, two bright patches staining her cheeks as she started for the kitchen. 'Our children are far more important than old grievances!'

Her hands were unsteady as she removed the casserole. Then she almost dropped the plates when Ailsa rapped on the glass of the back door. 'Mum! You're back — where on earth did you rush off to this morning?'

'Town. Got to the main post office just before closing,' she explained breathlessly, her pleased expression changing to concern at Dorrie's tense face. 'What is it, pet? There's not been bad news from the hospital? Or about Izzie?'

'Oh, no, nothing like that, thank heavens,' she said hastily. 'Graham and I have had words.'

'I can guess what about.' Ailsa passed her a long brown envelope. 'You'd better give him this, then.'

'Your savings!' exclaimed Dorrie, looking inside. 'We can't take this, Mum!'

'Yes, you can. You must.'

'Oh, Mum ... ' she whispered gratefully. 'Graham will be so relieved. But *you* must give it to him.'

With Dorrie at her heels, Ailsa went into the living-room where Graham was slumped at the table, trying to absorb the legal language of the finance company's notification.

'It isn't much,' began Ailsa quietly, sliding the envelope on to the table. 'But it'll bring the van payments up to date — and there should be enough left to tide you over until you get paid from Chadwick's. I only wish it could be more,' she finished ruefully, touching his broad shoulder sympathetically.

'I don't want your money!' Graham exploded angrily, almost knocking over the chair as he lurched to his feet. 'It's bad enough I can't provide for my wife and family, without taking hand-outs from my mother-in-law!'

He thrust the envelope back at Ailsa and strode past her from the room. With a shocked glance at her mother, Dorrie rushed after him into the hall.

'What's the matter with you?'

'I still have my pride, if nothing else!' Grabbing his jacket, he wrenched open the front door. 'Can you not understand that?'

'Graham!' she called, following as he marched away down the path. 'Where are you going?'

'To work — for all the good it'll do!' he shouted over his shoulder, unlocking the van. 'I'll be back about four.'

'Wait!' she cried, but the telephone began to ring, freezing her in her tracks.

Dorrie hesitated as the van's engine fired, then turned and half-ran indoors. A familiar fear clutched her heart as she snatched up the receiver.

'Mr Hamilton! What is it?' she blurted, instantly recognising his voice. 'Is something wrong with the twins?'

★ ★ ★

Graham got as far as Chadwick's factory gates before the impact of what had just happened hit him hard. How could he have rowed with Dorrie at a time like this? And throwing Ailsa's kindness back into her face that way! What had he been thinking of? Suddenly, everything seemed to overwhelm him.

Starting up the van again, Graham drove aimlessly around town before making for the loch where he and Dorrie had often walked while they were courting. There he sat for the rest of the afternoon. He headed home in good time, expecting to find Dorrie and Ailsa bustling around making ready to go to the hospital and collect Tom. But the whole house was silent and empty.

It was only then that Graham recalled the phone ringing as he'd driven away hours earlier. What if it'd been the hospital? Suppose Tom's tests . . .

'Graham? Is that you?' Dorrie's voice drifted downstairs. 'Can you come up?'

'What's — ?' He halted on the landing, staring through into the nursery.

Dorrie was standing there, her face wreathed in smiles as she cradled Tom in her arms. 'Look, Tom!' she whispered to the babe, her eyes never leaving Graham's astonished face. 'Look — your daddy's home!'

Graham stared at his wife and son. He'd never confessed it to Dorrie, but there'd been many times he'd almost given up hope this day would ever arrive.

'Aren't you going to hold your son?' said Dorrie with a smile, raising the drowsy infant to Graham's arms. 'Don't be afraid to cuddle him, love — he won't break!'

Graham just nodded, letting Dorrie steer him to the rocking-chair. Tom's wide blue eyes fluttered open and then closed again, as he nestled deeper into Graham's jumper.

'Is he all right? He seems awfully still.'

'He's just been fed. He's sleepy.' Dorrie perched on the edge of the ottoman to watch the two of them together. 'He'll probably be wide awake all night and keep us up!'

'I won't mind,' said Graham gruffly, beginning to rock gently in the chair, his gaze resting upon the contented bundle in his arms. When he did look up, he saw that Dorrie's eyes were wet.

'I wish Lucy was home, too,' she whispered in a small voice.

'She will be soon, you'll see.'

'It was dreadful having to leave her behind at the hospital this afternoon,' went on Dorrie brokenly. 'She was watching us. When she saw us taking Tom, and she started to cry . . . I asked Mum to stay with her a while.' Dorrie swallowed a sob, reaching out to touch Tom's tiny curled fingers. 'I didn't want Lucy to feel we were abandoning her.'

'Calm down, love. She'll be fine,' persisted Graham, his forehead creasing. Dorrie was far from being herself these days. She always looked washed out, and she'd never been weepy like this before the twins were born. 'Lucy's getting stronger every day — Nurse Petrie told us that, didn't she?' After a minute, he added, 'How come you went and brought Tom home earlier than expected, anyhow?'

'Mr Hamilton had to stand in for a colleague at the clinic this afternoon, so he phoned to ask if we'd collect Tom straight after lunch,' explained Dorrie absently, tucking the shawl Isobel had crocheted more snugly around Tom's toes. 'I phoned Chadwick's to try and let you know, but you weren't there.'

'I ended up at the loch. Everything seemed such a mess. I just didn't know what to do for the best, but . . . ' Graham's gaze slid from her to Tom, and across to the two cradles he'd made. 'Would Ailsa still be willing to lend me that money, d'you think?'

'She wouldn't take it back,' Dorrie said softly. 'It's in the bureau — and it *isn't* a loan. Mum said it's yours to do with as you think best, Graham.'

He shook his head fiercely. 'No, it'll

only be a loan. You have my word on that. I'll repay every penny as soon as I can.'

She glanced at him questioningly.

'I'm not giving up — at least, not until after I've been and talked to Jim. You were right, Dorrie. There's nobody else who can possibly help me out with the work I've got on.' He sighed. 'I never did tell you what happened between the pair of us, did I? Not what happened, *exactly* . . . '

She said nothing, realising the bitterness between himself and his elder brother was very difficult for Graham to talk about.

'The croft had been in our family for generations. Mother and Dad loved the land, but Jim and I didn't,' he began soberly. 'We both wanted a different kind of life. Jim had plans to be a builder. Me — I had no plans. I just wanted to get away from the croft. By the time I left school, Mother and Dad were getting on. Dad's health wasn't so good, and Jim had already given up his apprenticeship to work on the croft. He wanted me to change my mind about leaving home, and stay so we could work together on the land. Make something of the place. Well, I hated the idea! As soon as I left school and got fixed up with a job in town, I upped and left Jim to it.'

'I do wish you'd told me all this before.' Dorrie gently covered his hand with her own.

'Jim had no choice. He took care of Mother and Dad, looked after the croft, and kept everything going on his own,' related Graham bleakly. 'Dad was too ill to . . . I should have stayed at the croft, Dorrie! Helped Jim out, and been there with Mother and Dad at the end. I never even showed my face — I just walked away and hoped things would sort themselves out somehow!'

'I truly believe you should get in touch with your brother,' murmured Dorrie. 'If for no other reason than to tell Jim he has a niece and a nephew.'

'I suppose I could write and try

explaining things,' sighed Graham, at a loss how to begin bridging the years of hostility and separation. 'Tell Jim I'd like to come up and see him? Although I'll not blame him if he tells me to get lost!'

★ ★ ★

Graham got no answer at the croft-house when he arrived at Kincarron the following Friday. Pushing his hands into his pockets, he wandered across the cobbled yard, glad to stretch his legs after the long drive, and curious to look around.

The place was much as he remembered. Shabbier, though. The croft obviously hadn't been worked for years, and the stone byre was partially converted into a two-storey cottage. Graham was peering inside through one of the grimy windows when he heard a car approaching. Glancing around, he saw Jim Nicholson turning into the yard driving a taxi.

'You're a cabby now,' was the only thing Graham could think of saying as his elder brother strode towards him. 'You'll be working mostly in Inverness?'

'Beats struggling on this place,' replied Jim dourly. 'I'm my own boss. But it could be better. You look well enough,' he continued, starting past Graham to the croft-house. 'And your wife and family?'

'Doing fine. My boy Tom's settled in a treat at home, and we expect wee Lucy out of hospital soon,' responded Graham enthusiastically. 'What of yourself?' he asked more soberly as he followed Jim indoors. 'Are you wed?'

'I was going to be — Moira Ross. But that was years ago when Mother and Dad were alive. Moira wanted me to leave the croft and move to town; become a builder like I'd always planned . . . ' Jim paused, as though he'd already revealed more than he'd intended. 'What's past is past, Graham. It's the future we've both to look to. There's no sense beating about the bush. You need my help to finish your factory job, and I need an extra pair of hands up here. I've had to sell off most of the land piece by piece, so there's only the croft-house and the byre left. I'm doing them up to sell them.' He took a key from the hook by the croft-house gate. 'Come outside. I'll show you how far I've got converting the byre into a dwelling.'

Half an hour later, Graham was standing considering the interior of the stone byre. 'You're talking about months of graft!' He shook his head doubtfully. 'Granted, between us we've tackled most kinds of jobs, but we're not proper builders, Jim. Nor electricians or plumbers, either.'

'Any specialised work's already done. The conversion only needs finishing off,' argued Jim impatiently. 'What do you say? Yes or no, Graham?'

'But it'd mean me living up here! Being away from home,' he hedged desperately, his mind back at Auchlanrick with Dorrie and the babies. 'Be reasonable, man! I've a family to think about.'

'My labour now, so you get your contract with Chadwick's finished on time — for *your* labour later.' Jim faced his brother in the byre's shadowy light. 'That's my offer. Take it or leave it.'

★　★　★

The days since Ortega's battle-scarred troops commandeered the train had settled into a peculiarly orderly pattern. Travelling around the clock, they steamed further and further from the border and back toward the capital city. Routine stops were made for fuel and water and for local people to board and alight.

Although heavily armed, the soldiers paid little attention to their fellow passengers. Douglas, Isobel and the others could easily have slipped away from the train — if they'd had the energy to attempt escape. Instead, Isobel wearily tended the wounded soldiers, while Angela and Luis rarely emerged from the boxcar where Cesar Bernaldez was resting. The frail old man sometimes didn't even recognise them as they strove to make him as comfortable as the oppressive heat and the train's lurching motion allowed.

'Just because none of them look older than twenty doesn't mean you can get careless, Karl,' remonstrated Sam when they were clambering back aboard the train after taking on coal. 'Young as they may be, they're armed and dangerous.' He cast a backward glance to where soldiers in grimy uniforms with weapons slung carelessly across their shoulders were sauntering about the rail-stop, drinking beer, smoking cheap cigars, and eyeing up the local women. 'Mentioning Luis in their hearing like you did — you could have got him and the old man captured or killed!' he went on scathingly. 'It's lucky that lad didn't understand a word of English.'

'It was a slip of the tongue, OK?' the

professor retorted irritably. 'The soldier *didn't* know what I'd said, so no harm was done.' He sank heavily onto one of the wooden seats and watched Angela pass along the corridor for a breath of air. She practically ignored him these days, spending all her time with Luis Rosales.

'Karl, are you listening to me? Right now, these soldier boys haven't a clue who we are,' persisted Sam testily. 'But they've watched their comrades fight and die and they're scared, bitter and full of fire and hate for the enemy. There's no speculating what they'll do — to all of us — if they ever find out the only son of President Rosales is one of us — ' Sam broke off, his attention caught by Luis's sudden appearance in the corridor. Although less than five yards away, he walked blindly past the two men and straight to Angela Lennard.

'He's dead, Angelina.'

'Oh no,' she whispered. Señor Bernaldez's death was not unexpected, of course, but . . . Angela reached up, touching Luis's ashen face. 'I'm so very, very sorry.'

'Cesar . . . ' Luis faltered, sorrow constricting his chest. 'He — he was thirsty. I went for water. I was gone only a few minutes, but when I got back . . . '

'My condolences for your loss,' interrupted Sam brusquely, stepping forward. 'Now you must concentrate on saving your own life. We'll say nothing about Cesar's death until the train's about to pull out. By then, the soldiers will have drunk enough to be more amenable,' he concluded calmly. 'If they agree to stay here overnight to organise a burial, that will give you plenty of time to get away. By daybreak, you can be long gone.'

'No!' exclaimed Luis, his hand clasping Angela's. 'I wish to attend Cesar's funeral. And what about Angelina's safety? Do you imagine I would ever leave her here? Or do you believe I'm a coward?'

'You still don't get it, do you, Luis?' cut in Sam brutally. 'You're a danger to the rest of us!'

'He's right, Luis,' murmured Angela. 'When this train gets to Castildoro and we're forced to give ourselves up, it'll go easier for us if they think we haven't seen you since the plane wreck. You've been wanting to fight for your country's freedom,' she urged gently. 'So go do it!'

'We should all go,' he argued gravely. 'If Cesar's passing gives us this opportunity to escape, then we should take it. All of us together.'

'We'd never make it, Luis,' replied Douglas simply. 'I'm not sure how much more Isobel can take. For her and me, at least, returning to Castildoro is the best option. You must see that?'

Luis inclined his head in acceptance. 'I'd like to be with Cesar for a while. Excuse me.' He turned, and Angela immediately accompanied him, linking her fingers through his.

None of the three men spoke

immediately. Cesar Bernaldez's death had touched each of them.

'You should go with him, though,' said Douglas unexpectedly, glancing at Sam. 'Enrique Soler said they were searching for you, too. Ortega would love making an example of you. This could be your only chance of staying alive.'

★　★　★

Three days after Cesar Bernaldez's burial, the train approached a sizeable town. As Douglas, who was driving the train, braked to draw alongside the station, he saw an army Jeep, flanked by armed motorcyclists, waiting on the dusty timber platform.

'Reception committee. None other than Enrique Soler,' he said over his shoulder. 'Fetch Isobel and Angie up here, Karl. I don't want them alone when the troops board.'

Soler jumped from the Jeep, signalling for Douglas and the others to alight. When they were lined up on the platform, he grinned humourlessly. 'Destiny is indeed capricious, Doctor Blundell! Our paths continually cross. Get in.' He indicated the Jeep. 'I have orders to escort your party directly to General Ortega.'

'We're British and US civilians,' protested Douglas, well aware that resistance was futile. 'You have no authority over us.'

Soler raised his shoulders in an indifferent gesture, indicating the ranks of armed troops. 'I believe I have all the authority necessary. Come quickly, please. General Ortega is not a patient man.'

They sat, two facing two, on the benches in the Jeep's open rear section. While Soler drove, the soldier in the passenger seat turned to watch them, his rifle levelled across the seat-back. The Jeep gathered speed, pulling clear of the station with the motorcyclists riding parallel on either side. Isobel sat hunched beside Douglas, her eyes downcast. Anxiously, he gripped her limp hand.

'Don't worry. They're deliberately trying to intimidate us.'

Karl leaned closer to ensure his words couldn't be overheard. 'Wonder how Sam and Luis are doing?'

'They'll have made it!' mouthed Angela decisively. 'Luis knows the mountain country very well. Oh, no — Look!'

As Soler swung down the curving road into the outskirts of Castildoro, evidence lay everywhere of the fierce struggle that had taken place in the sleepy city before it finally fell to Ortega. Houses were razed, and whole blocks burned out and abandoned. Two bullet-pitted tanks had been abandoned close to the church gardens, and further ahead the rubble of the bank was crumpled into a gaping crater.

'Where is everybody?' exclaimed Karl loudly. The streets were deserted except for patrols of soldiers in grimy battle-dress green.

Soler glanced around into the rear of the Jeep and shrugged. 'Castildoro has a strictly enforced curfew.'

Government House had been taken over as the military headquarters, but Soler drove past the imposing building. Increasing speed, he left the city behind and headed out into the rolling countryside beyond. Eventually, Angela recognised the route.

'This leads to Casa Rey!' she exclaimed. 'I've spent vacations there. The owners are friends of my parents.'

'Quite correct, Miss Lennard.' Soler glanced at her in the rear-view mirror. 'The hacienda was for many generations the summer home of the Aragall family. General Ortega has established his personal household at Casa Rey.'

'What's happened to Señor Aragall and his wife?' demanded Angela. 'Where are they?'

'In prison,' responded Soler indifferently, as the lights of the hacienda glimmered between strands of shadowy trees.

★ ★ ★

The Jeep, with its escort of motorcyclists, passed between ornate iron gates into a courtyard heavy with the scent of oleander and thickly fringed with magnolia trees. As it drew alongside an elegant arcade, a tall distinguished man emerged from the tiled portico.

'Good evening! I am Gualterio Ortega. Welcome to Casa Rey,' he greeted them graciously. 'Please, come inside.'

They stepped into a cool marble-paved hall. Its walls were of extravagantly carved red mahogany, and soft lamplight spilled from numerous niches and alcoves. Classical music was drifting through the open doors of the library, and hovering in an archway beyond the sweeping staircase was a small middle-aged woman dressed entirely in black.

'Febe will show you to your rooms. You will naturally wish to rest and freshen up after your long journey. Perhaps later you will join me for dinner?' Ortega continued. 'Meanwhile, if you require anything, do not hesitate to ring. I'm most anxious your stay at Casa Rey be as pleasant as possible.'

There wasn't anything they could do but follow the housekeeper up the staircase.

'I'll bring tea presently.' Febe paused at one of the doors and pushed it wide. 'Doctor and Mrs Blundell, this is your room.' She flicked a switch and lamps sprang alight on the cream-washed walls of the wide, long bedroom with its tall shuttered windows.

Despite the circumstances, Isobel gasped incredulously as her gaze swept the exquisite tapestries and hand-woven rugs, the painted ceiling, the graceful Spanish renaissance furniture and damask-upholstered chairs. After everything they'd been through, to have finally come face to face with the man they so feared and find themselves surrounded by beauty and opulence was nightmarish. Her knees buckled and she sank on to the corner of the huge bed. Then her gaze found the open wardrobe — their clothes were hanging neatly inside.

'Douglas,' she mumbled, getting up to run her hands over the dresses and skirts, 'I don't understand. These clothes — they're ours! We had to leave them behind. How did he get them?'

'From the plane wreck, I suppose. And from our room at the hotel.' Douglas frowned, wrapping his comforting arms about her. 'Ortega's obviously gone to a great deal of trouble to arrange this, but why? What on earth is he up to?'

Douglas was not to find out until much later that evening. He and Isobel had bathed and changed, and Febe had brought the promised tray of tea. He persuaded Isobel to rest a while, and was sitting beside her while she slept, when Febe noiselessly returned and Douglas was politely summoned to the library. Music was still playing, strident and bellicose now, but tuned to a low volume.

'Ah, Doctor Blundell!' exclaimed General Ortega genially, glancing around from the drinks cabinet. 'I adore Wagner, don't you?'

'Not particularly,' retorted Douglas, distractedly waving aside the sherry Ortega was offering and meeting the man's eyes steadily. 'Get to the point, can't you? Why have you brought us here? What do you want from us?'

★ ★ ★

'He's coming from Paris at midnight!' echoed Janey with a sigh, watching Kirsty fussing around making ready the spare room at Chimneys. 'That's *really* romantic!'

'Josh is a romantic man.' Kirsty's eyes were sparkling as she put a gift-wrapped bottle of his favourite aftershave lotion onto a pile of clean towels in the dresser drawer. 'I'm delighted to say!'

'Of course. He's half-Italian, isn't he?' mused Janey wistfully. 'Italians are very passionate!'

'Is that right?' said Kirsty with a grin, flicking Janey's thick fringe with her fingertips as they started downstairs. 'I'll have to take your word for it! Actually, I'm a bit nervous about this weekend,' she confided candidly. 'Josh and I lead such different lives now. It's months since we even saw one another. What if we've changed?'

The back door burst open and Teddy began barking ecstatically. There was a clamour of excited voices and running feet and paws thundering along the hall.

'Oh, no! Paul and the boys are back already!' groaned Janey. 'I wanted you to set my hair!'

'I still will,' promised Kirsty, jumping down the last few stairs to be instantly surrounded. 'How's the newspaper business, boys?'

'The printer let me press the button!' Robbie shouted, tugging on her sleeve, his chubby face upturned. 'We put the paper to bed!'

'That's newsroom talk,' explained Paul with a grin.

'I knew that!' she returned airily, but her eyes were solemn when they met Paul's above the boys' heads. He'd promised to contact the Foreign Office again today, and Kirsty's spirits plummeted at his slight negative gesture. She bent, putting her arms about both Alasdair's and Robbie's shoulders. 'There's milk and Mrs Bell's famous toffee buns waiting for you in the kitchen — but only one each! Save the rest for your camp-out this evening.'

She straightened to find Paul watching her and smiling. The warmth in his eyes took her by surprise. 'What?'

'Nothing.' He shrugged, still smiling at her and thinking — not for the first time — how very much Kirsty had changed recently. She looked so right here now, with a family gathered around her. 'Oh, I almost forgot. We met the postman in the lane. Package for you. I had to sign for it, so it must be important.'

'I'm not expecting anything.' She took the padded bag and scrutinised it.

'Hurry and open it!' urged Janey. 'It might be a present!'

'It's a complimentary copy of *Wuthering Heights* — the audio novel I narrated for Josh's recording company!' exclaimed Kirsty, her face lighting up as she unwrapped the illustrated book-shaped box. 'Doesn't it look nice?'

'Mmm, very nice,' remarked Paul. 'My mother adores the Brontës. She belongs to the society at Haworth.'

'Kirsty could've played Cathy on TV,' Janey announced rather grandly. 'Her agent said the boss of a big new series wanted her to be the star!'

'They're planning a serial of *Wuthering Heights*,' explained Kirsty dismissively. 'Apparently the producer heard an advance copy of the audio novel and knew my theatre work, so he approached Ruth, my agent. I probably wouldn't have actually *got* the part anyway.'

'Bet you would!' declared Janey loyally, starting back upstairs again. 'I'll go and wash my hair.'

'OK, give me a shout when you're ready.' Kirsty moved toward the kitchen, glancing at Paul. 'Can I get you a coffee, or do you need to get back to the paper?'

'Yes, please. And no,' he replied. 'What's the point of being the boss if you can't play truant occasionally? Kirsty, before we join the boys,' Paul added hurriedly, 'would you like to visit Haworth? It's a fascinating place, and I'd enjoy showing you around.'

'That would be nice,' she answered carefully, keeping the tone light. 'Isn't there a railway museum somewhere nearby? Alasdair and Robbie would like that. And exploring the Brontës' home might even inspire Janey to read a book.'

'We can turn it into a family trip, by all means,' he agreed readily. 'But if Winifred Bell will mind the children, I rather hoped you and I might have a day out together. Just the two of us.'

'I couldn't do that, Paul,' she refused softly. 'I know in many ways we're closer than ever before, but you must understand Josh is the most important person in my life now.'

'You're too impulsive. Too emotional. Everything's always all or nothing with you.' He shook his head, meeting her eyes with thinly disguised exasperation. 'And quite frankly, I think you're far more committed to the relationship than he is.'

Paul realised, even as he spoke, that it was the worst possible moment to have this out with her. However, he couldn't now leave unsaid what had been in his mind for weeks.

'If Josh Elliott loved you as much as you think — *hope* — he does, he wouldn't have gone abroad and left you when you needed him most.'

'That's not fair!' Kirsty was stunned by Paul's bluntness. 'Josh has a career to think about.'

'You had a career, but you gave it up when the people you loved needed you.'

'Mine was a different situation entirely,' she returned. 'Opportunities were opening up at the Paris studios for Josh. He'd have been crazy to turn them down.'

'Not in my view,' countered Paul curtly. 'All right, so his staying in Britain might have meant a sideways career move, but he could've done it if he'd wanted to. If I've upset you, I'm sorry,' Paul concluded regretfully, his attitude softening. 'But I want you to see things as they are, Kirsty — not as you'd wish them to be.'

★　★　★

With the exception of Janey, who scorned camping out when you were only pitching your tent in the garden, the family spent that afternoon wandering back and forth with all the necessaries for Paul and the boys' forthcoming night under canvas. Paul himself was in the cellars, searching for a missing piece of camping stove, when the ring of the telephone brought him up for air.

'Kirsty!' he yelled from the garden doorway, waving her up from the beck's bank. 'Phone!'

'Is it Paris?' she queried breathlessly, sprinting indoors. 'Josh?'

He nodded, disappearing back down into the cellar.

'Josh! I *knew* it'd be you,' she began almost shyly. 'Only seven and a bit hours to go till we're together!'

'We're having nothing but problems here, sweetheart,' he said without preamble. 'There's no way I'll make my flight this evening. Sorry.'

Usually they'd talk for hours, but suddenly there seemed nothing left to say. Besides, Josh had to get back into the studio.

Kirsty held on to the telephone long after the line from Paris had gone dead. Suddenly she became aware Paul was standing beside her.

'I couldn't help overhearing,' he murmured awkwardly, stretching out a hand to touch her shoulder, then withdrawing. 'I know you were looking forward . . . ' His sentence tailed off. Paul paused, studying the stove he was holding. 'I can see to the boys, if you want.'

'No, I — I'm all right. Thanks, anyway,' she faltered. Paul's sympathy was far more upsetting than his criticism. 'I'll be out in a minute.'

He nodded again, walking along the hall to the garden. Kirsty squeezed her eyes tightly shut and expelled a ragged breath, disappointment and apprehension churning in the pit of her stomach.

Josh wasn't coming tonight. And he hadn't said when — or if — he *would* be coming.

★   ★   ★

As it was arranged for Winifred to watch over everything at Chimneys the next day, Kirsty decided to spend her unexpected free time usefully. She caught the early train to collect the remainder of her belongings from the London flat she, Josh and Gwen Taylor had shared.

Gwen was still dancing in summer season at Rhyl, and although they got along well enough, Kirsty was relieved she wouldn't be seeing her flatmate. She wasn't up to fending off Gwen's chatty inquisitiveness, especially where Josh was concerned.

Wearily, she climbed the three flights from the street. Although the flat wasn't anything like as comfortable or as cosy as the wee house at Auchlanrick where she and her sisters had grown up, the place was still Kirsty's home, and giving it up this way was painful. From now on, she wouldn't have anywhere to really call her own. Her last piece of independence was gone.

She was about to put her key into the lock when the door swung open. Gwen and Josh stood framed in the doorway. They looked as astonished to see Kirsty as she was to see them. She took an involuntary step backwards, noticing that Josh was freshly shaven, the edges of his hair damp from the shower.

'Kirsty!' he exclaimed, recovering

first. 'Gwen and I were going for breakfast — '

'So I see!'

'I reckon Gwen ought to make herself scarce!' Gwen chuckled, kissing Kirsty's cheek. 'Shame you've had to give up your room, Kirst. It's rotten luck. See you later!'

Josh closed the door behind her, catching Kirsty's sleeve when she would've walked straight past him into the lounge.

'Sweetheart . . . ' he murmured, drawing her back against him and circling her with his arms, his lips unerringly locating the racing pulse-beat at the base of her throat.

Kirsty stood rigid, numb inside, unable to return Josh's caresses.

'What's wrong?' he asked, turning her around to face him.

'Nothing.'

'Nothing?' he echoed sceptically, searching her eyes. 'I know you too well to believe that.'

'I — I was surprised to find you

here,' she managed to get out, alarmed at the direction her thoughts were taking. 'With Gwen.'

'She's in town for a pantomime audition at the — ' Josh broke off, continuing with dawning realisation. 'That's it, isn't it? It's Gwen! You think she and I — '

'No,' blurted Kirsty untruthfully, averting her eyes and trying to pull free, but Josh's strong hands were still gripping her arms. 'I don't think that.'

'Of course you do,' he retorted in disgust, finally setting her free. 'It's written all over your face!'

'Well — what am I supposed to think?' she retaliated defensively. 'Last night you told me you had to stay in Paris!'

'I *did* stay in Paris. We worked all through the night and I got the first flight back this morning. There was nothing directly into Leeds, so — ah, what's the point?' he demanded scathingly. 'Trust should run both ways, Kirsty.'

'What does that mean?' Her challenge was indignant.

'You saw me with Gwen and immediately suspected the worst,' he retorted bitterly. 'Yet for months, I've had to accept that you've been seeing more of a former boyfriend than you have of me. Whenever you phone or write, it's 'Paul said this' or 'Paul did that'!'

Kirsty's shocked eyes widened. 'Paul's the children's godfather. He comes to Chimneys to see them, not me!'

'Get a grip on reality, Kirsty. The man still loves you!'

'That's nonsense,' she snapped. 'Paul's a fine man. A friend! Nothing more.'

'Are you absolutely sure about that?' countered Josh icily.

'I'll fetch my things.' Pointedly breaking their eye contact, Kirsty turned to go into her room. 'That's why I came here today.'

'You've a lot of stuff. Why not leave half of it in my room?' he suggested with brittle politeness, following her and leaning against the door frame. 'Collect it next time you're in town.'

'I won't be coming down here again.' Kirsty didn't look at him or pause from frantically pushing her belongings into bags. She was desperate to get away from him, to get out of the flat, to be on her way home.

'If that's how you want it,' commented Josh evenly, his quiet politeness more disturbing than anger. 'Run back to him — I'll even drive you to Euston!'

'There's no need — '

'Oh, there's every need.' He gripped Kirsty's wrist tightly, stopping her hasty packing. 'I'm not about to make it easy for you. I want you to think!'

She drew breath to reply, but words wouldn't come. His eyes were staring into hers, and Kirsty saw exactly what Josh was remembering: that other day he'd taken her to the railway station, and kissed her for the very first time. A strangled gasp escaped her. Kirsty blinked hard, lowering her head, feeling again the vivid emotions that kiss had stirred within her.

'What's the matter?' Josh demanded, pulling her closer and tilting her chin so that she would look up at him. 'Memories too tough to face? Surely not!'

His mouth came down hard upon hers for an instant, then he released her and turned on his heel. 'Let's go. You don't want to miss your train!' he muttered sarcastically; and, snatching up her luggage, he strode out.

Kirsty heard the flat's door slam. He was gone. She'd lost him. It was over. Standing alone in the silence of her old room, the tears she'd earlier denied streamed unnoticed from her eyes.

9

After they'd explored the old church and museum at Haworth, Paul took the boys for ice-cream at the village teashop while Kirsty and Janey lingered on at the Brontë family home. Kirsty slowly followed her niece down the straight neatly-edged path, pausing at the gate to look up at the square stone parsonage where Charlotte, Emily, Anne, and Branwell had spent much of their short lives.

'Queer to think of them sitting in that little parlour writing their books, isn't it?' mused Janey, smoothing her fingers across the copy of *Wuthering Heights* she'd bought from the museum's shop. 'You seemed miles away when we were looking around. Were you thinking about playing Cathy in that TV serial?'

'A little,' admitted Kirsty as they

turned the church corner and started down the steep cobbled street into the village. 'But mostly I was thinking about your mum and Dorrie and me. It's been years since we've all been together with Mum.'

'D'you think Gran'll come back from Scotland to look after us again?'

'She can't. Dorrie still isn't strong,' replied Kirsty simply. 'Besides, one new baby takes a lot of looking after, but Dorrie has to divide her time between caring for Tom at home and being with Lucy at the hospital — so you're stuck with Paul and me!'

Janey laughed, then her eyes clouded. 'There hasn't been any news for ages, has there?'

Kirsty shook her head, slipping an arm around the teenager's shoulders. 'Paul's always trying to get more information, but he hasn't had much luck lately.' She paused. 'It doesn't mean anything's happened, just that news isn't getting out.'

Janey gave a resigned sigh, not

speaking again until they were strolling past the Black Bull, when the display in a nearby shop window caught her attention. 'Oh, wouldn't Mum love that!' She pointed to a handmade quilt. 'You know how she likes old-fashioned things.'

Kirsty stopped to admire the quilt's traditional patchwork design. 'Do you want it?' she asked impulsively. 'To give to your mum and dad when they get home? From you, and Alasdair and Robbie?'

'It's terribly expensive. Can we really have it? queried Janey tentatively, her eyes shining. 'It'll be a welcome-back present for them from us, won't it?'

'My sentiments exactly!' declared Kirsty enthusiastically, linking her arm through Janey's and tugging her towards the shop's doorway.

That evening at Chimneys, Paul came downstairs after seeing both boys into bed and found Kirsty stuffing the day's shorts, socks and T-shirts into the washing machine. 'Want a drink?'

'Please. There's some white wine in the fridge.'

He filled two tall glasses before joining her on the doorstep, where she was standing watching the soft early-evening colours of the late summer sky. 'Thanks.' She smiled up at him, sinking down contentedly onto the step. 'Are the boys settled?'

'Robbie was asleep before his head touched the pillow. Alasdair's trying to read, but he can hardly keep his eyes open,' chuckled Paul, squeezing down beside her on the sun-warmed door-stones. 'It's been a good day, hasn't it?'

'The best.' She sighed, drawing in a deep, slow breath of the soft, sweet September air. 'It was the perfect way of rounding off the summer holidays for the children.'

'They *did* enjoy it, didn't they?' Paul stretched out comfortably, gazing across the vivid heather to Hawksbeard Crag, its ragged edges glowing golden with drying bracken. 'I've always envied Douglas,' he said meditatively. 'Having Isobel and the children. Without a wife and family, a real home and proper roots, true happiness just isn't possible.'

Kirsty glanced at him a shade warily, but his eyes held a faraway expression and he wasn't looking at her. They sat in companionable silence until the sun dipped beneath the horizon and its afterglow trailed streaks of tangerine, blue and crimson across the sky.

'Robbie asked me if his mum and dad will be back to take him to school,' she murmured, frowning. 'All the other little ones will have their mums or dads with them on their first day. I'm worried it will be upsetting for him.'

'We'll take Robbie together, Kirsty. Starting real school is a huge step for any child. If there are problems, we'll cope with them — together. I promised I'd be here for you and this family . . . and I will,' he reassured her quietly, hesitating before reaching out to smooth a straying wisp of hair from Kirsty's forehead.

Conscious of the touch of his hand, and its meaning, Kirsty met Paul's eyes regretfully. 'I'm sorry, Paul. I like you . . . and I care for you . . . But I can't be more than a friend. I — ' she faltered, loth to hurt him, yet wanting to speak plainly so there could be no misunderstanding. 'I miss Josh so very much! Not a single day passes that I don't think about him. It breaks my heart when I remember all we once shared — and everything we've lost.'

Paul held Kirsty's troubled gaze, his hand light and comforting against her cheek. 'You and I used to be much closer than friends. I'm sure we could have a happy and contented life together — but I do realise it's still far too soon for you to consider that,' he added quickly when she drew breath to speak. 'I can wait. I asked you to marry me once before, Kirsty. When the time's right, I'll ask you again.'

★ ★ ★

The days after the children returned to school seemed long and empty for Kirsty. Summer vanished overnight into constant rain, and even Chimneys seemed cold, dismal and very empty.

Despite the weather, however, Kirsty took long walks with Teddy along the beck in a vain bid to shake off her feelings of isolation and loneliness. She found herself looking forward keenly to Paul's visits and the days when Winifred came in.

'I need a part-time job, Win!' she called from the pantry one wet Friday when they were baking pies for the harvest festival. 'Do you know of anything I could do?'

''Fraid not. I could ask around, though.'

'I'd be grateful. I've been independent since I was about Janey's age. Even a wee job would help! But it isn't only for the money,' she confessed, emerging with the trug of cooking apples. 'I *need* to work. I've felt so . . . restless. Chimneys is my home now, and I honestly believed I'd settled down, and yet ... Oh, I can't even explain it!' She grimaced exasperatedly. 'Goodness knows what's come over me. Maybe it's this endless rain and being cooped up on my own day after day. I haven't been right since school started up again.'

Winifred gave the younger woman a knowing look. When she'd met Paul the morning after he'd taken Kirsty and the children to Haworth, he'd related every last detail of their outing. And, watching his open, sincere face while he talked, Winifred had understood a great deal more. 'You've not heard from your young man these past weeks, have you?' she asked unexpectedly.

'Josh? No, I haven't. And I don't expect to, Winifred. A clean break was the only way,' replied Kirsty sombrely.

'It's queer how things have a habit of turning out for the best,' remarked Winifred evenly. 'You're lucky, Kirsty. You've your whole life ahead of you, and you haven't to look further than your own doorstone to find a chap who's devoted to you.'

Kirsty half-smiled, her eyes lowered as she rolled out the pastry. Paul was in London, harrying his contacts at the Foreign Office yet again, and she'd been surprised at how much she was missing him. 'Paul tried to warn me about my relationship with Josh, you know. We even quarrelled about it. I was sure he was wrong — and I told him so! But despite that, he's been incredibly understanding these past few months. Paul's changed since I first knew him. Mellowed, somehow.'

'Happen it's *you* who've changed. Maybe Paul Ashworth's been the right one all along, and it's taken till now for you to realise it. He's a fine man, Kirsty, and he loves you dearly. Let him go a second time,' cautioned Winifred, 'and you'll regret it for the rest of your life!'

★ ★ ★

'Graham's as pleased as punch about finishing Chadwick's on time and at being able to pay you back so quickly, Mum,' said Dorrie as they cut sandwiches and filled tea flasks for the brothers' long drive north to Kincarron. 'I know you meant that money as a — oh, look!'

She was looking through the window to the garden, where Jim Nicholson had been raking leaves. He'd gone across to the twins' pram, retrieving the blanket Lucy had kicked off, and was tucking it back gently around the sleeping babies.

'Jim's so good with them,' went on Dorrie affectionately. She'd grown fond of Graham's elder brother and couldn't help feeling he'd had a rough deal from life. 'I hope he meets somebody nice and has a family of his own someday. He's such a kind man, yet he seems so alone — ' She broke off as Graham came downstairs with his suitcase. 'Are you sure you've got everything, love?

'Aye, just about.'

Wanting to give the couple time

alone to say their farewells, Ailsa dusted off her hands on her apron. 'I'll pop out and tell Jim you're ready to set off.'

'Thanks, Ailsa.' Graham returned her smile, but his expression sobered when he looked at Dorrie. 'You're sure you'll be able to manage while I'm gone?'

'With Tom and Lucy home, and getting bigger and bonnier by the day? Of course I will!' she insisted cheerfully. 'You're not to be worrying about us!'

Graham nodded, pulling on his jacket. 'I'd never have finished Chadwick's without Jim helping me,' he began. 'And I've really enjoyed working with him, you know. We were chalk and cheese years ago, when we were lads, but now . . . Him and me rub along together grand, just like brothers should do. He's a good sort, Dorrie. And I've been thinking about the twins' christening,' he added hastily, hearing Jim and Ailsa coming in from the garden. 'What d'you think about Jim — '

Dorrie was beaming. 'Tom and Lucy couldn't have a finer godfather!'

The weather was cold but dry, and the brothers were working outside from first light until dusk every day. Then they'd go indoors to put in few extra hours on the interiors of the old stone byre and the dilapidated croft-house.

'We're doing all right here,' commented Jim, surveying their progress late on a sleety November afternoon when he returned from Inverness with another vanload of building supplies. 'It'll be a real good job when everything's done.'

'I've a mind to dig out these cobbles around the croft-house,' remarked Graham, shouldering the lengths of wood and striding across the yard from the van. 'With bulbs and suchlike planted, it could be an attractive little garden by spring.'

'There's plenty of space at the back for the sort of vegetable patch Mother had. And for a big family garden, too,' agreed Jim. 'Graham, why don't you go home this weekend? Your bairns'll be up and running around if you leave it much longer!'

'It *has* been a while.' He grinned. 'Are you coming with me?'

'No, I'd best get the taxi out and earn a pound or two,' Jim replied ruefully. 'Will you and Dorrie be fixing a date for the christening?'

'Dorrie's set her heart on waiting until Isobel and Douglas come back from South America,' said Graham with a frown. 'She wants both her sisters there in church.'

'You can't blame her for that. Has there been any news?'

'Not a word, as far as I know,' he replied grimly. 'I've not said anything to Dorrie, of course, but I can't help wondering if they'll ever get back. Or even if they're still alive.'

The brothers continued unloading the van in near silence, the sleet soaking their hair and clothes. They tramped back and forth across the cobbled yard until Jim finally put into words what he'd been mulling over in his mind for days.

'By right, this croft belongs to both of us. That's the way Mother and Dad would have wanted it. You've put in a lot of hard graft, Graham, especially on the croft-house. If you'd fancy living there, well — it'd be a grand place for a family.'

Graham's heart thumped, his dream of providing a home of their very own for Dorrie and the twins at odds with what he believed to be fair. 'I'm grateful,' he began quietly. 'But I made my choice all those years ago, Jim. I left. Whatever the croft brings is yours — that's only right.'

'The proceeds of selling the byre cottage will be enough for me,' Jim countered firmly. 'And if you've any worries about your business, Inverness is bound to offer decent prospects for a first-rate painter and decorator.'

Graham didn't answer. He paused in the byre's open doorway, gazing across at the croft-house's trim roof and neat windows. Dorrie would love it, he was certain. But would she agree to move from Auchlanrick, leaving her mother living there alone?

★ ★ ★

On the spur of the moment, Josh took the afternoon flight from London to Edinburgh, hired a car, brought a road map and drove north to Auchlanrick. It was only when he'd actually reached the village and found Ailsa Carmichael's home that he began wondering if he was doing the right thing. Then he spotted an elderly woman leaving the house with a twin pram and was out of his car in an instant.

'Mrs Carmichael!' he called, approaching Ailsa at the gate. 'We've never met. I'm Josh Elliot, a — friend of Kirsty's.'

'I know who you are,' she returned stiffly. Although it wasn't in Kirsty's nature to pour out her heart to her mother, Ailsa was well aware how badly hurt she'd been when her relationship with this man ended.

'Nothing's happened, has it?' she demanded suddenly. 'To Kirsty?'

'What?' queried Josh blankly, momentarily confused. 'No. No, she's fine as far as I know. I haven't seen or heard from her for several weeks, but Kirsty *is* the reason I'm here, Mrs Carmichael. May we talk, please?'

'I can't invite you indoors, Mr Elliot,' returned Ailsa curtly, wheeling the pram through the gate and into the lane. 'My daughter had a sleepless night with the babies and she's trying to rest. I don't want her to be disturbed.'

'OK.' Josh shrugged, falling into step beside her. 'I only got back to London from Paris this morning, and while I was having lunch I bumped into Ruth Goodman, Kirsty's agent — ' He broke off while Ailsa exchanged a few words of greeting with a neighbour.

'Mrs Carmichael, are you aware there's to be a new television adaptation of *Wuthering Heights*?'

'My granddaughter mentioned something about it.' Ailsa stopped at the pillar-box, checking through several letters before posting them.

'Ruth Goodman told me the serial is casting shortly, and both the producer and director greatly respect Kirsty's past work.' Josh's exasperation increased still further when Ailsa bent to fuss with the pram's hood. She didn't seem to be listening to a word he was saying!

'Don't you realise how important this is?' persisted Josh impatiently. 'The leading role will almost certainly go to Kirsty — if she tries for it!'

'Kirsty's grown up at long last. She's finished with all that acting nonsense!' snapped Ailsa. 'She's putting down roots, making a proper life for herself.'

'You don't understand her at all, do you?' he cut in emphatically, distractedly pushing his hand through his hair. 'The only reason Kirsty's abandoned acting is because she has to look after her sister's children! Look, I didn't come here to cause trouble, Mrs Carmichael. I just wanted to make sure you appreciate exactly how much Kirsty is having to give up,' persisted Josh earnestly. 'If you were to go back to Yorkshire, she would be free — '

'There's no purpose discussing this,' replied Ailsa reasonably, turning the pram into the newsagent's. 'Somebody has to be at Chimneys looking after the children, and I can't possibly do that. My daughter needs me here.'

'Kirsty is your daughter, too!' Josh's hot temper finally ignited. 'And right now, she's about to make yet another sacrifice for the sake of her family. Think that over, Mrs Carmichael — you might like to do something about it!'

★ ★ ★

Douglas leaned away from the computer screen and removed his glasses, massaging the bridge of his nose between thumb and forefinger. He'd had no choice but to accept General Ortega's ultimatum — but that didn't make working for the dictator any less agonising.

Ortega was determined that the excavation at Castildoro should continue, and he needed Douglas's archaeological expertise — along with his contacts amongst private collectors, universities and museums all over the world. For although the Inca, Spanish, and Portuguese artifacts being recovered from the site might not be glamorous, they were extremely valuable. There was a thriving black market — which Douglas despised — in such treasures, and selling them to the highest bidder would provide finance to arm, feed and clothe Ortega's army. Even the general's promise of freedom for Isobel and the others couldn't appease Douglas's conscience.

Despairingly, he rose and crossed the office on the hacienda's ground floor. Opening the shutters, he gazed out across the sunlit garden with its dancing fountain and shady groves of magnolia. Angela Lennard was strolling along one of the paved paths from the direction of the stables. She was chatting and joking with a small boy as she helped him carry a heavy basket of fresh fruit up to the hacienda.

It amazed Douglas how easily she'd adapted to captivity at Casa Rey. She hung around the kitchen and stables, gossiping with Febe the housekeeper and the other servants who had once worked for the Aragall family. On impulse, Douglas strode out into the hot, heavily fragrant garden. He was staring blindly into the gushing waters of the fountain when Angela joined him.

'You look awful,' she said. 'And that's being tactful.'

'Thanks,' replied Douglas wryly. 'I saw you going out earlier. Have you been riding again?'

'All the way to the electrified fence. *That* wasn't here when my folks and I used to come visit the hacienda for vacations with the Aragalls.' She glanced around to see where the nearest guard was posted. Ortega had kept that portion of his promise at least. They

were treated as honoured guests here —
but they were constantly watched, and
an armed member of the general's
personal staff was never far away.

Angela bent to the fountain, idly
trailing her fingers in the splashing
water. 'Ortega's on his way back.
Should be here before nightfall.'

'How do you know that?' Douglas
exclaimed, then shook his head apologetically. Angie never admitted where
she got her information. He half-
suspected she'd somehow made contact
with the local resistance who were
passing on intelligence. 'You and the
others will be going home then,' he
commented instead.

'We'll need to be careful,' she
continued, carelessly dabbing her face
with the fountain's cool water. 'Ortega's
taking heavy losses of men and
equipment in the hills, and last night
one of his munitions factories was
sabotaged. Douglas, I realise how hard
it will be for you, but you must agree to
anything — everything — Ortega

demands! Don't risk antagonising him,' she concluded, her casual attitude a stark contrast to the urgency of her warning. 'At best he'll change his mind about sending us home. At worst, he'll kill us!'

★　★　★

It was with a heavy heart that Isobel finished packing. She couldn't bear the thought of leaving Douglas. When her suitcase was ready beside the bedroom door, they simply stood there together, waiting for Febe to knock and tell them it was time to go. A truck would take Isobel, Angela and Karl to the military airfield.

'Douglas, I promised you — and myself — that whatever happened, we'd never be separated,' she murmured, her arms folded tightly as though she were cold. 'If it wasn't for the children, I'd never have agreed.'

'You have to go, Isobel.' He kept his tone calm, tenderly stroking her hair.

He hated the notion of trusting her safety to a ruthless despot like Ortega, and dreaded the prospect of watching her go aboard that plane at the airfield. 'Once you're home at Chimneys, everything will be back to normal for Janey, Alasdair and Robbie — that's what's important.'

'Normal?' Isobel was aghast. 'Without you home with us?'

'You'd have gone home alone after your holiday anyway,' persisted Douglas practically. 'I had another eighteen months' work to do at Castildoro. And that's precisely what I'm doing — working at the dig,' he concluded. 'I'm useful, Isobel. Ortega needs me, so I'm not in any danger whatsoever. You must make the children understand that.'

They heard Febe's soft footsteps approaching along the landing, and Douglas moved to embrace his wife for the final time. Although Ortega had granted him permission to see her off at the airfield, these last few moments alone were precious. Douglas felt her burrowing her face into his shirt front, knew she was crying, and his own vision blurred. He drew Isobel still closer, rubbing his cheek against the softness of her hair. It was time to say goodbye. Would this be the very last time he'd ever hold his wife in his arms?

★ ★ ★

Karl, Angela and the other five archaeologists were already seated on the timber benches in the windowless rear section of the military truck when Douglas helped Isobel climb inside. Hardly a word was exchanged as the heavy vehicle rumbled over rough tracks towards the airfield. Everyone was mightily relieved at being released from captivity — but terribly afraid their freedom might be snatched away at the last moment. And nobody could forget one of their number would not be boarding the plane — Douglas would be compelled to travel back in the empty truck to Casa Rey.

'Isobel, remember — I *will* be coming home when this is over,' whispered Douglas against her ear. 'And never forget that I — '

His words were drowned by a burst of gunfire close to the truck. The heavy vehicle braked violently, lurching and swerving to a juddering halt. Douglas couldn't see what was happening, but more shots, the rattle of automatic weapons against metal, the smashing of glass, cries, and a barrage of shouts and orders in several languages terrified him, and he pulled Isobel close. The truck's rear doors were wrenched open, and a heavily armed young man wearing camouflage fatigues stood there. His eyes narrowed as he tried to penetrate the dimness of the vehicle's interior.

'Do not be alarmed, my friends.' His earth-smeared face creased into a white, humourless smile. 'Ortega has stolen much from our country — but now the resistance is doing a little commandeering of its own!'

'Luis!' Angela was first to recover, almost stumbling from the truck to reach his side. 'I thought you were never coming!'

'You should have had more confidence in us, young lady!'

Sam Fraser strode around from the front of the vehicle. He was wearing the battle-dress green and twin stars of Ortega's generals, and paused at the truck's open doors to consider its startled, silent passengers. 'Lost for words, Doctor Blundell? That makes a pleasant change.' He grinned. 'But we've no time for chit-chat anyway — we've got to get this truck turned around and on its way!'

'Away from the airfield?' queried Douglas at once. 'But Isobel and the others are flying home! Ortega's cleared it.'

'I'd have been disappointed if you hadn't made at least one objection.' Sam gave a short laugh, but his eyes were unreadable when they briefly met Isobel's. 'You *do* want to go back to Yorkshire with your wife, don't you, Doug? Then shut up and do as you're told.'

'Sam and Joachim there will drive you to the border,' Angela explained hurriedly, indicating one of the half-dozen uniformed men milling watchfully about. 'One particular checkpoint is poorly guarded. A battle-scarred army truck under the command of a general will get through unchallenged. Once over the border, you'll be met by someone from the British Consulate.'

'You're not coming with us?' cried Isobel in horror.

'I belong here.' Angela moved closer to Luis's side. 'I never intended to leave.'

'We'll contact your families,' promised Douglas as the truck's engine throbbed noisily into life. 'Let them know you're both all right.'

'Goodbye, and good luck!' Angela had to shout to be heard, reaching up to grasp their hands. 'When peace comes, perhaps we'll meet again!'

'Hurry up!' bawled Sam from the cab, revving the engine even more impatiently. 'If we don't get a move on, we'll never get across that border!'

★ ★ ★

'We're safe and well, Kirsty!' Isobel's voice rang out joyfully over the crackling line. 'We're on our way home!'

The phone call came in the middle of the night, and Kirsty went racing around Chimneys rousing Janey, Alasdair and Robbie from their beds to talk to their mother and father.

During the next thirty or so hours, the telephone was rarely silent. There were more calls to and from South America, to Dorrie and Ailsa in Auchlanrick, and to Douglas's elderly parents in Canada. And to Paul Ashworth, who'd quietly taken charge of the practicalities.

On the wintry November morning

Isobel and Douglas were expected home, Winifred stood at the kitchen table at Chimneys. 'I know it's only half-past seven, and Paul's not collecting them from Leeds until ten,' she muttered, sprinkling a generous scoop of cherries into her cake mix. 'But if I don't keep busy, I'll do nowt but fidget!'

'I'm hopeless at waiting, too,' agreed Kirsty with feeling. She and the children had been awake, washed, dressed and breakfasted long before six o'clock. They'd tried to pass the hours by playing Snakes and Ladders — Robbie's choice; but when his heavy eyes gradually closed, the game was quietly abandoned.

Janey had tiptoed upstairs to arrange the new quilt they'd bought during their day out at Haworth and place a bowl of freshly cut chrysanthemums in her parents' room. Alasdair gladly braved the chill, foggy morning and disappeared for an early walk along the beck with Teddy.

Kirsty eased a cushion under Robbie's head, stretching him out more comfortably on the couch and tucking a rug snugly about him. 'He'll probably sleep for hours now!' she whispered, joining Winifred at the kitchen table. 'I'll wash my hands and help you.'

The garden door crashed open, and Alasdair burst inside with Teddy barking ecstatically and tearing around his legs. 'They're here!' he yelled breathlessly, his cheeks scarlet with happiness and cold. 'Mum and Dad are back!'

Janey galloped downstairs, Winifred dropped a bowl of brown sugar, and Robbie awakened with a start, wondering what was going on. His sleepy eyes widened as Paul shepherded Isobel and Douglas inside, their tired, drawn faces wreathed in smiles. The whole of Chimneys erupted into a commotion of cries and hugs and laughter and questions. Everybody was talking at once, shouting to make themselves heard. Then, quite unexpectedly, there was a moment of stillness, of realisation, of unspoken thanks.

'Everything's just the same, Douglas,' murmured Isobel, gazing almost disbelievingly at him. 'We're home, and everything's just the same as always. Winifred's even baking for Christmas, just like always!'

'Aye, well, I've never been one for leaving things till the last minute,' retorted the elderly woman gruffly, wiping her eyes with the corner of her apron. 'Sit yourselves down now, and I'll put the kettle on. I daresay you're parched for a decent cup of tea.'

Kirsty crept from the kitchen, leaving the family alone. Paul followed suit, joining her in the hall.

'They had the option of an earlier flight.' He was beaming. 'Decided to surprise everyone.'

'Isn't it wonderful having them back?' she laughed, then half-turned. 'Oh, goodness! I'd better move my stuff from Douglas's study. He's bound to — '

'Don't run away, Kirsty!' exclaimed Paul impulsively. 'I have tried to be patient, but there'll never be a better day than this one to ask you — '

'Please, Paul,' she whispered sorrowfully, raising imploring eyes. 'Don't.'

He bowed his head regretfully; pain, disappointment and futile longing a leaden weight in his chest. 'I only want your happiness,' he murmured. 'You know that, don't you?'

'Yes.' She swallowed the knot of sadness in her throat. 'I do.'

'What will you do now?' Paul enquired at length. It took a monumental effort to concentrate on matters safe and mundane. 'Stay on here?'

'I'm not sure. I haven't a home of my own now, or a job.' She glanced at the closed kitchen door, heard the muffled sounds of the family's laughter, and was suddenly sharply aware she had a life, as well as a career, to rebuild. 'I've no idea what, or where, my future is going to be, Paul,' she admitted honestly. 'And it scares me.'

The whole family gathered at Chimneys for Christmas. Only Douglas's parents, who were too frail to make the long trip from Quebec, were absent.

'It's a shame they couldn't have been here, but when Isobel and Douglas take the children over to stay with them for a little holiday next month, it'll make up for it a bit,' Winifred remarked to Ailsa as they bustled around preparing for the Hogmanay celebrations.

The last day of the year had dawned crisp and clear, with bright December sunshine glittering on the frozen beck. The two women had Chimneys to themselves, except for Douglas and Harry Bell, who were in the study continuing a chess game they'd started on Christmas Eve.

Isobel and Dorrie had strolled to the station with the twins to meet Kirsty off the train. Paul and Graham were skating with the boys on the beck, and Janey had dashed into town to buy a pair of spangly earrings.

'After they get back from Canada,' went on Winifred, carefully pressing Isobel's best embroidered tablecloth, 'will you be moving into Chimneys?'

'I'm really considering it,' Ailsa confided, pausing from slicing oranges and lemons for the punchbowl. 'I couldn't have left Auchlanrick before, but now that Dorrie's hale and hearty again, with a family of her own, and she and Graham have the option of that beautiful croft-house at Kincarron . . . '

Her gaze strayed through the window and away to where Paul was gliding along the ice, towing Robbie behind him on his tiny skates. 'I only wish *Kirsty* was settled down! Paul Ashworth was such a good influence on her, Winifred, and I really had such hopes they'd . . . But there, as soon as Izzie and Douglas got home, she was off and away,' Ailsa sighed heavily. 'I gather she's practically living out of a suitcase in Birmingham now, you know. And look what happened at Christmas — Kirsty came for the one day, then rushed straight off again!'

'She didn't have much time to prepare for playing Cathy,' replied Winifred loyally. Although *Wuthering Heights* would mostly be filmed in the television studios at Birmingham, the outdoor scenes were being done in and around Haworth and the Brontë parsonage, so Kirsty had been rushing back and forth as well as continuing to study the novel and the script. 'She's been working really hard this past month,' Winifred reminded Ailsa mildly. 'Kirsty's very dedicated.'

'Hmm. It's what she wants, I suppose,' conceded Ailsa, her eyes still wistful as she watched Paul with the children. That man would make such a fine husband and father! 'But this acting business isn't a bit what I'd have chosen for her.'

★ ★ ★

310

Isobel, Kirsty and Dorrie had gossiped the entire way home from the railway station, stopping off for hot chocolate and a muffin at the inn. The sisters were in high old spirits when they clattered into Chimneys late that afternoon.

'She's here!' announced Isobel, relieving Kirsty of her bobble hat, coat and fluffy scarf. 'Kirsty's back!'

'But not for long!' Dorrie chipped in cheerfully, going through to the fire-lit sitting-room and lifting Tom from the double Moses basket while Kirsty cuddled Lucy. 'The film folk have been waiting to do a snowy-morning scene at the parsonage, so Kirsty has to go back to Haworth and work.'

'Surely not?' exclaimed Ailsa, disappointed and more than a little vexed. 'It's Hogmanay, after all!'

'That's rotten luck,' sympathised Alasdair.

'You'll miss the party, Auntie Kirsty!'

'Enough, everybody!' Laughing, she halted the children's protests with outstretched hands. 'The driver's not collecting me until after midnight, so we'll all be together to ring in the New Year!'

★ ★ ★

After midnight, the festivities at Chimneys quietened and the family settled around the fire while Paul spun a spine-tingling tale about a headless horseman who haunted the nearby woods along the beck. Kirsty caught Isobel's eyes, raised a finger to her lips, and slipped away. Hogmanay had made her reflective, and she wanted a little time alone before the television company's driver called for her. Wandering from the house, she drifted down the garden and out along the beck. The frozen water and snowy banks were frosted and sparkling beneath a hazy silver moon.

'Kirsty!'

The familiar voice stopped her where she stood. Turning slowly, she saw Josh striding along the bank. He halted a few yards from her. Whole seconds of tense silence ticked away as they stared at each other, unsure what to say or do.

Josh cleared his suddenly dry throat. 'I went to Haworth. They told me a driver was coming here to collect you. It wasn't difficult persuading him to let me take his place, not on New Year's Eve.'

Kirsty nodded wordlessly, startled by the rush of pure happiness singing through her at the very sight of him.

'How have you been?' he asked.

'All right,' she got out shakily, scarcely able to breathe. 'You?'

'Fine. No, *not* fine!' he corrected vehemently, catching her shoulders with both hands and closing the distance separating them. 'I've never felt so miserable in my life!'

'It wasn't that I didn't trust you, Josh,' she mumbled unhappily. 'I — I just couldn't help being jealous.'

'I understand — now,' he confessed ruefully, smiling at her for the first time.

'It's torn me apart, imagining you up here with another man — even one who's just a friend. I didn't want him seeing and being with you when I wasn't.'

'We've — ' she began, but Josh's fingertips against her lips silenced her.

'Right from the start, there's only been you, Kirsty. I've never wanted — never loved — anyone like I love you,' he breathed. 'I don't know what the future's going to be, or how we'll organise our lives. All I *do* know, is whatever lies ahead, I want us to share it.'

Kirsty smiled, gazing up at him. 'It's a new year,' she whispered, reaching up to brush his lips with her own. 'A time for new beginnings!'

He gathered her into his arms, and presently they started back along the moonlit beck, casting but a single shadow upon the glistening snow.